I AM NOT
JACKSON POLLOCK

I AM NOT
JACKSON POLLOCK

JOHN HASKELL

FARRAR, STRAUS AND GIROUX
NEW YORK

Farrar, Straus and Giroux
19 Union Square West, New York 10003

Distributed in Canada by Douglas & McIntyre Ltd.
Printed in the United States of America
First edition, 2003

Frontispiece photo credits: Image of Janet Leigh in *Psycho* courtesy of M.P. & T.V. Photo Archive; images from *The Seventh Dawn, Exstase, Touch of Evil, My Life to Live, Chimes at Midnight, The Third Man,* and *Psycho* (Anthony Perkins) courtesy of Photofest, Inc.; images of Glenn Gould and *Sputnik* dog courtesy of Archive Photos/Archive Films; image of Jackson Pollock and image from *The Passion of Joan of Arc* courtesy of Everett Collection, Inc.

Library of Congress Cataloging-in-Publication Data
Haskell, John.
    I am not Jackson Pollock / John Haskell.— 1st ed.
      p. cm.
    ISBN 0-374-17399-0 (hc : alk. paper)
      1. Artists—Fiction.   I. Title.

    PS3608.A79 I13 2003
    813'.6—dc21

                       2002033889

Designed by Jonathan D. Lippincott

www.fsgbooks.com

10 9 8 7 6 5 4 3 2 1

The author would like to express his gratitude to the institutions that encouraged the writing of this book—the MacDowell Colony, the Corporation of Yaddo, the New York Foundation for the Arts, Dixon Place, Big Dance Theater—and to his friends and family who made the writing possible.

For my father, John Haskell,

and my aunt, Harriet Haskell

CONTENTS

DREAM OF A CLEAN SLATE

I am not Jackson Pollock. I should say I am not Jackson Pollock, the famous artist, when he walked into the Cedar Tavern and there was a girl sitting in a booth at the back of the bar and he wanted to go to her. So he did. I should say he *started* to go to her, but he was feeling a thing he called nervousness, a feeling in his body that he didn't like, so he stopped at the bar for a drink, a whiskey. After the whiskey he was still feeling the nervousness, so he had another drink. But the feeling wasn't going away; in fact it was becoming more intense and distracting and when he tried to control it, by holding it in or down, his body would rebel against him, and against itself, and all he knew to do was have another drink, a whiskey, and a beer to go with that, and a whiskey to go with that, and a beer to go with that . . .

He's standing, leaning his elbows on the bartop, and the distance between where he's standing, with his empty glass, and where the girl is sitting, with her dark hair, expands, like an expanding universe. She's getting farther and farther away, and part of him—his desire—goes to the girl, and the rest of him stays at the bar, drinking and trembling. And as the distance between where he is and where he wants to be expands, he finds he's getting farther away, not only from her, but also from himself, or that part of himself that would act on his desires. They're not bad desires—they're simple desires—but they're frightening because they involve another person who may or may not like him. He smells like beer and Camel cigarettes and she may or may not like his smell. So he stays where he is, fixed in space, and reacts, not to his own trembling, which he hates, but to the girl, who he sees as the source of his trembling. "Who is she?" he thinks. "She's nothing. She's some . . . nothing. I'm Jackson Pollock. I'm the greatest living painter in the world." But this attempt to obscure or deny the feeling he doesn't want to feel, doesn't work. He's standing at the bar, with his elbows dug deep into the barwood, watching her, not going near her, but looking at her and waiting, wishing that she would do something, hoping that she would get up and do something to relieve his stupid pain, although it isn't pain exactly, but something like it, and he doesn't like it, and he wants her to take it away; he wants her to stop what he's feeling. And she isn't doing it. She isn't doing anything. So he thinks, "Fuck her."

Jackson Pollock dreamed of a clean slate. He tried to free himself from the past so that he could begin at the beginning and paint what he wanted to paint—a thing he called "the unconscious." He said, "The source of my painting is the unconscious," and he wanted to paint, not just about, but with this thing. He wanted to break through to this thing, to poke a hole in the fabric separating him from it, and that's what he did. That's what he painted. Not the hole in the fabric: his struggle was not finding a language to merely describe the hole; his struggle was to tear at the hole and open the hole and go into the hole, and that's what he did. And from there he splattered his paint on the canvas.

He was attracted to the unconscious thing because he had an unconscious or unknown or chopped-off part of himself. He didn't want it known because he didn't want it taken away. Anything known, he felt, would be taken away. Every time he painted a painting it was taken away by the shit-ass critics and collectors who left him with nothing, except the desire to change what was happening. Painting was a way to change, not only the world, but the way he was in the world, and that's why he cultivated, not desire, but something like desire, something inside of him that would eat at him until either he or the world was different.

He had a dream I think, and in the dream he walks out of the Cedar Tavern, stands on the sidewalk, looks out onto the street, and the black pavement of the street becomes the ocean. When he turns around the tavern is gone. His friends are there, standing on the pier, drinking and laughing, and they're looking into the water. He looks into the water, and he can see in the water the thing that he wants. He doesn't know what it is because the water obscures his vision, but he knows he wants it. There's a rope coiled up by his foot and he takes that rope and he ties one end around an old wood piling and the other end he ties around his stomach, with a good solid knot. Then he jumps into the water and he dives down. But the water is dark, and he can't see so he has to feel, with his hands, for the thing that he wants. But the rope is too short. So he comes up for air. Standing again on the pier he looks around and his friends are taking off their pants. They're putting on swimsuits, laughing, their voices far away. Behind them, a seagull, perched on the cab of his dad's gray pickup, watches him with one eye. The bird shits, jumps up, and then flies through the air. And Jackson thinks, I am a bird, and he unties the rope from his waist, and holding the end of it in one hand, he dives like a bird into the water. With his other hand he reaches out to feel for the thing he wants. But he can't feel it. He can't feel anything. And he hates that. He wants to feel something. He wants to feel the thing that he saw was there. He saw. It was there. He would like to let go of the rope and reach out . . .

He staggered into the Cedar Tavern. This was 1956 and the girl, whose name was Ruth, was standing at the end of the bar, full-figured, dark-haired, and looking at him. Lee, his wife, was sitting at a table. He walked to the bar, to a point equidistant between the two women, and started drinking himself into a state of numbed oblivion. At a certain point Ruth walked over, sat on the stool next to him, and began asking him questions about who he was. He wasn't comfortable talking about himself so instead he talked about Pollock, the artist, the greatest one, according to the magazines. He explained to her, not *his* position, but the position of Jackson Pollock after he'd painted his drip paintings. He had discovered this language that let him say what he wanted to say, that let him get his unconscious out and down on the canvas. And that's what he did. That was good. And he continued doing it because it was what the language let him do. He could get his unconscious out and down and with purity too, but sometimes purity is not enough, sometimes you want something more, and he was saying that Pollock wanted more and needed more and needed to be given more, and as he told her this, gesticulating with his hands, he touched her lightly on her arm. And he could feel her respond, and smile. So he continued. About how Jackson Pollock tried to find a new language. He'd spent a lifetime making the hole and getting into the hole and now he wanted to get out. But he was stuck. And his old language, which had been a good language at one time, wasn't working; it wasn't giving him the satisfaction or fulfillment he'd gotten when he opened the hole for the first time, went into the hole, and splattered the paint exactly where the canvas wanted it. Now he was saying he hated the canvas. And Ruth was rapt. She was listening intently, absently placing wisps of hair behind her ear. And as he was telling her about the violence and passion of the man named Jackson Pollock he could see out of the corner of his eye his wife getting up to go, and she was mad, he could tell, and he said, "Hold on," to Ruth and he walked outside to catch up with Lee. They'd been breaking up for a number of years so he knew her well enough to know that she'd be walking back to their room. But when he got outside she wasn't walking anywhere. She was standing right there on the sidewalk, her hands on her hips, right on the corner, waiting. She was an artist and so she had that fiery vein of emotionality right below the surface, and now it was right *on* the surface, open and flowing, and she was yelling, "What the fuck are you doing to me?"

"I'm not doing anything."

"Well you're doing a pretty good job."

"What?" he said. "What do you want me to do?"

"Why don't you just forget it," she said.

"Forget you," he yelled at her.

That's when she turned and walked away.

"Forget you," he said after she'd left. After she'd been gone a long time he was still standing there. He was still saying, "Forget you."

Jackson was troubled, no doubt about it, but he had to get on with his life. He staggered back into the Cedar Tavern, and there was Ruth, not at the bar anymore, now she was sitting at her table and he wanted to go to her. And he did. He stopped at the bar and had a couple of quick drinks, but he did in fact go to her table. He sat with her and yes, he was nervous. He felt the thing in his chest that was bigger than his chest, expanding under the ribs of his chest, and he felt that he could easily explode. He began arranging the salt and pepper and ketchup on the table. He was hoping she would do something or say something or want some thing so that he could give it to her and get the feeling over with.

But she did nothing.

So here was a man about to explode and a woman who was quite happy. Ruth was a twenty-five-year-old artist, or artist's model, who still found New York exciting. Life, men, adventure; they were all synonymous for her, and so she loved the Cedar and the famous artists she'd barely heard of, but they were famous, that was the main thing, and the one she was sitting with was the most famous. So she was happy.

Jackson, on the other hand, was dying. He thought if he would just explode, if he would go ahead and burst into a thousand pieces, it would at least be better than the feeling of wanting to explode, and being unable to. He tried to sit there and live with it, but after a while . . .

"I'm Jackson Pollock," he told her.

"I know," she said.

"I'm the world's greatest living artist."

"You don't have to do anything," she said. "Just be yourself."

"Be myself?"

Jackson couldn't accept the fact that she could accept him. It made no sense. He looked at her and what he saw was someone who was petite and dark and pretty. He saw someone with large breasts like his mother, although she didn't remind him of his mother. His mother was gigantic. Ruth was not gigantic. Ruth was . . . smiling.

"Be myself?"

He wanted to be himself. He didn't want to be Jackson Pollock the Artist, but it wasn't that easy. First of all there was his fear of what might happen if he would be himself, which, when he imagined it, felt like falling through weightless space—which he didn't like. And then there was the chair he was sitting on. He was sitting on a wobbly chair. The legs weren't level on the ground, so he stood up, walked around behind Ruth, and he sat on the other side of the table, on another chair.

Ruth, however, continued looking at the chair he'd been sitting in before.

"Hello?" he said.

But she didn't seem to hear him. Or didn't want to. Or maybe he wasn't speaking the right language. She was still looking at the other chair.

"Come on," she said. "Let's go." But she said it, not to Jackson, she said it to the place where Jackson *had* been sitting, as if she didn't realize that he wasn't there anymore. She was talking to where he once was, seeing the person that used to be there, waiting for him, but that wasn't him.

"I'm here," he said. "This is me."

But she was oblivious. She was looking at the old part, the false part, the part he hated. That's who she was embracing. She reached out and took that false part by the hand and said, "Come on, let's go."

Jackson whispered to himself, "Don't go." And he stopped.

"Come on," she said, "let's go."

"Don't go."

"Come on," she said.

"Don't go . . ."

Finally she took him by the arm and led him to the door. You could see them standing in the doorway, putting on their coats, first one arm, then the other. She was taking him back to her apartment but she was taking the wrong man. "She thinks she's taking me, but that's not me," he said to himself. "This is who I am. Here. This is me."

Jackson Pollock is usually either depressed or pissed off, and now he's pissed off. Yes, he's the possible greatest living artist, etcetera, but it doesn't feel that wonderful. Not to him. Yes, he goes home with Ruth and spends the night with her, but she thinks that he is someone else. So he's frustrated and dissatisfied, and his anger is looking for a target. He staggers into the Cedar Tavern and there's a mirror along the wall behind the bar, and as he walks along the bar, looking into the mirror, he can see Franz Kline, the abstract expressionist painter, and he thinks that Kline is watching him. He walks up behind Kline and says to him, "What? What are you looking at?"

Franz Kline is a man with a long fuse. He slowly turns around. "Knock it off, Jackson," he says.

"Fuck you, Kline. What do you want?"

Jackson is mad and he wants to get madder. If he can get mad enough the feeling he doesn't want to feel might go away. For a while. He doesn't want to be near this feeling or touch this feeling. If he touched it, even with a ten-foot pole, he would break down and he can't break down because he's an artist, all-American. If he touched it he would cry and he can't cry so he hits Franz Kline on the top of the head.

Kline looks over his shoulder but to Jackson's disappointment he doesn't respond. This drives Jackson deeper into his knot—a knot he loves, by the way—a knot filled with frustration, and he's looking for frustration when he makes some remark about the woman sitting next to Kline, some remark like, "Who's the bitch?"

"Stop it, Jackson," Kline says.

"Stop it?"

He can't stop it. He's locked in his struggle and his struggle is with the entire world. Franz Kline just happens to be the person sitting in front of him. He believes he would like to have a regular drink like a regular guy but really he wants to fight. He wants to fight the world, and Kline, knowing this and not wanting to indulge him, turns around on his stool, turning his back on Jackson.

Jackson, however, will not be unindulged, and he grabs Kline by his thick hair, pulls him off of the stool and onto the floor.

Kline takes his time getting up. He stands, turns, pulls back his arm, and launches a fist into Jackson's gut. Jackson doubles over and falls to the floor. Finally he gets what he wants. He's lying on his back in the spilled beer and cigarette ash, and looking up to Kline he says, "You don't hate me do you? Don't hate me."

These words sound incongruous, like non sequiturs, but if you'd hung out at the Cedar Tavern and if you'd known Jackson Pollock, the words would be very familiar. He wanted the frustration and he wanted the struggle and he wanted the fight, and at the same time he was reaching out. In his own way he was reaching out . . .

Jackson lived for a while on Long Island, with Lee, near a place called Springs. It was an old farmhouse and they'd been working on it for years. One day she called to him— she was in the bedroom and he was in the bathroom and she yelled in—"Would you bring me my shaving kit." It was a leather shaving kit and he brought it into the bedroom. She was lying back on the bed and she said to him, "Open it."

He tried to open it.

"Open it," she said.

"I'm trying," he said.

"Open it," she said.

But the zipper was stuck.

"I want something in there," she told him.

"I know," he said.

"I want something in there," she told him again, so he took a razor blade, cut the leather along the zipper, folded back the flaps, reached in and, "Yes," she said. "That's good."

He felt some shaving cream in there, and toothpaste, and he forgot what she wanted because she was smiling with her big white teeth in a way he'd seen before. He put the leather kit on the foot of the bed and he must have been smiling too as he spread her spreadable arms and legs and she was pliable, and she was saying the same words over and over. "That's good," and "Yes." She was saying, "Oh yes, oh yes, oh, oh," repeating that "Oh" until it lost whatever meaning it had and became only sound, and the sound had a meaning and the expression on her face as she made the sound, that had a meaning, and pretty soon she stopped even saying the word. It wasn't necessary. She stopped saying "Oh" out loud but she kept her mouth in the shape of saying it. Her lips were silently saying "Oh. Oh," over and over. She was making the shape of "Oh" with her mouth.

And that was the beginning. They created this thing. It was part of their relationship, a product of their love, and it was a good thing too because it gave them a way of express-ing their love, and knowing their love, and it made them close. It bound them to each other. If they were at a party, say, all they had to do was look at each other. One of them would look at the other, make the shape of "Oh," and it was all they needed. They knew exactly what the other meant. So that was good.

But then Pee Wee died. Pee Wee was the little canary with a flattop hairdo that lived with them. When he died they searched around and found a nice, level, fairly garbage-free location behind the house to bury him. Lee was holding little dead Pee Wee in her hand and Jackson was digging into the earth with the heel of his shoe at a place they'd picked near a green sapling. He said he didn't need a shovel but the ground was hard so he'd picked up a broken piece of brick and was chopping at the earth with that.

Then a bum appeared from out of the weeds, a local bum whose bulbous stomach was stained with muddy rivu-lets of sweat. He stepped up to Lee, who wasn't digging, ex-tended his hand, and as if she had no choice she extended hers and there was Pee Wee, lying on his back, with his lit-tle feet sticking in the air.

Lee and Jackson looked at each other and they both made the shape of "Oh." They smiled because they knew exactly what it meant.

Jackson said to the bum, "Well, it's good to see you but right now we can't talk. We'll talk later. Right now we're trying to bury our bird."

But the bum didn't leave. So again they made the shape of "Oh," and then they knew what they had to do. They ignored the bum. They placed Pee Wee into the hole and covered it with dirt and twigs and pieces of broken glass, and a tin can top that was part of the garbage. With these things they made a little monument for Pee Wee. Of course the bum was still standing there, and the more they ignored him, the more he seemed determined to stay. But they didn't want him to stay. This was a private and personal occasion and a bum was not something they wanted. So they looked at each other and made the shape of "Oh."

But nothing happened. And because nothing happened they kept making the shape of "Oh." They thought that it would be enough. But it wasn't. But they saw no choice, so they kept on trying. They kept making the face but obviously there was a problem. And it wasn't the bum or the smell of the bum, the problem was the face. But they didn't know what else to do so they kept on doing it, they kept making this stupid face at each other. And they didn't know what it meant, or what they meant even by doing it; but they kept doing it, more and more, because they were feeling more and more separated, both from each other, and from what they wanted to happen. And it was no longer a good thing, this thing they had, it was a bad thing now, like a wedge driven between them, separating them from each other.

They knew they would have to talk about it and one of

them at some point said to the other, "Why don't you stop it?"

"I'm trying to stop it, why don't you stop it?"

"Well I'm trying to stop it."

"Well you're not doing a very good job, are you?"

"Well why don't you just forget it then?"

"Okay. Fine. Forget it."

"Fine with me."

"Great."

"Fine then."

"Fine."

"Fuck you."

So Lee and Jackson, in a way, were trapped. They were caught by this thing that they'd created, the thing that made them close. Because they'd created it and it was a part of them, they couldn't just stop it, or kill it, or cut it off. They couldn't just get rid of it, they didn't think.

When Jackson was a boy he lived with his mother and his brothers on a farm outside of Phoenix, Arizona. He was in the house one afternoon with his mother. She was sitting on the old sofa darning some socks, or sewing, and Jackson was walking back and forth in front of her, stomping his feet across the living room floor. He was the youngest of the brothers and his mother called him the handsomest; he was also the neediest. He needed something right then, from her, and he wasn't getting it. And in thinking of how he could get it he thought of his older brother Charles. Everyone respected Charles and admired Charles because Charles had a talent for drawing. Jackson, motivated by that example, found a piece of paper and a pencil and put the paper on the back of a book and sat down on the hardwood floor, his back against the sofa, and began to draw a picture. It wasn't a representational image of the farm or his mother or himself. It *was* himself. It was him. He had kept himself in or down or hidden for so long that when he finally let himself out he found he could easily get himself onto the paper. When he finished his drawing he turned to his mother, sitting on the sofa above him, and he handed the drawing to her. She took it, she looked at it, and then she said, "You should draw it out like Charles. Charles," she said, "can draw." Then she handed him the drawing and went back to her sewing. And he took the drawing, but he didn't take his eyes off her. He was looking at her face, and as he watched her face it started to become ugly and mean and deformed, and the more he watched it the more deformed it became until what he saw wasn't her face, it became a mask of her face, an ugly, grotesque mask, and he kept watching it, waiting, hoping that the ugly mask would fall away and that behind it a beautiful face would be revealed. But of course that never happened. There was no mask. The face was her face. It was ugly because Jackson made it ugly because he was mad. And because he was mad he jumped up and ran outside, into the yard. The farm was not a big moneymaker and there wasn't much more than dusty brown dirt and a lot of chickens running around, and a few scraggly trees. Another brother, Sande, was playing with a neighbor in the yard; they were pretending to be men. They had a big old axe and they were chopping wood when Jackson wanted to join them. But because he was the youngest one and the handsomest one they wanted no part of his little world. But he wanted a part of theirs. So he placed his finger on the worn wood of the chopping block and dared the person holding the axe to let him in. The person holding the axe lifted the axe so that it hung in the air above Jackson's head and Jackson kept his finger where it was, tempting the person to let the axe come down. And when it did come down it chopped off his finger—the end of his finger—which rolled off the chopping block into the dirt. A rooster came along, pecked at it, picked it up, and carried it away. And that was it. The finger was gone. And Jackson had his proof. There was his confirmation. Look at me, his missing finger would say, and look at what you've done. Look at the life that's falling apart, the drunkenness and the failure and the dissolution, and know that you're responsible. He needed the idea of that chopped-off finger. He pitied it and protected it and hated it for the rest of his life.

A final dream. He's standing in an open field with a bow in one hand, an arrow in the other, and a deer—the field is filled with tall grass—a deer enters the field, quietly eating at the grass. He places the arrow's notch in the cord, raises the bow, and aims his arrow at the heart of the deer. The deer raises its head, looks out with one eye, and Jackson lets go. He wants to let go. He wants to let go of the bowstring and have the arrow sail through the air, but when he releases his fingers, nothing happens. Nothing moves except the deer, who quietly passes from the field.

Jackson Pollock was bound to fail, but at least he would fail heroically. He'd made his name by fighting the way things were, and when he got famous he kept fighting the way things were, but since *he* was the way things were, he fought himself. Two opposing impulses dominated his life: the desire to reach out into the world and touch some thing, and the desire to keep that thing away. This was his struggle, and it felt like shit, and to get rid of the feeling he shook his head. That was his art. The paintings he saw hanging in the world were all the same old pieces of shit, so he shook his head. His greatness was realizing that what existed in the world didn't work for him, and then shaking his head to find the thing that did. And certain people, especially the people who paid him money and made him famous, they wanted him, expected him, and demanded that he keep shaking his head. They didn't want to shake their own heads but they were happy to indulge Jackson and encourage Jackson, because shaking head was good for business. And Jackson, in an effort to find something real and solid, shook his head. Which was what they wanted him to do, and the problem was, he didn't want to do what they wanted him to do, he wanted to do what *he* wanted to do, but because they wanted him to do what he wanted to do, what he wanted . . .

All he knew was to shake his head. But it didn't help. All it did was get him dizzy. And he wanted to get back. He felt he had to get back, to something, so he got in his car, a green Oldsmobile convertible, and drove. He was at a point A, on Long Island, and he wanted to get to point B, on another part of the island, so he got in his car. He wasn't alone. Ruth was with him, and she'd brought along a friend of hers from New York City, Edith, and they were driving to a party. Jackson had been drinking that day and was probably driving erratically, and Edith, in the backseat, was screaming for him to turn around. And when he did turn around she continued screaming. He was driving along, one girl next to him, petrified, the other girl in the backseat, screaming, and he was known for being decisive and he wanted to be decisive, and he wanted to change what was happening. He wanted to shake everything out of his head and start at the beginning. But this desire only made him dizzier.

And when the road made that one particular turn he tried to follow the road. He wanted to make the turn, and have the road and the car and the girls all make the turn together, with him. But the steering wheel, or the road, or he, was not quite right. Jackson Pollock wanted to turn and he tried to turn, and he did, he turned the steering wheel, but the car was going too fast or he turned too slowly or too late and suddenly he was driving along the shoulder, into the dirt, and when the car collided with a stand of saplings he was thrown from the car and sent sailing through the air. He could see down below him the road, and the horizon above that, and the sky above that, and above that a cloud, and the cloud had a face, an ugly, deformed face, and he watched as the face began to fall away. He let it fall away, and for an instant he could see behind it. And then he hit the tree. The tree didn't move so he died. And that was the end. It wasn't the beginning. You could see that he was dead, and that the girl in the backseat was also dead. That was the end. You'd have to be looking from some very great distance to see that that was the beginning.

ELEPHANT FEELINGS

1. TOPSY, NEEDY

This is about an elephant, electrocuted one hundred years ago. Her name was Topsy, and she was famous at a time when people were still amazed by an elephant. Plus she did tricks. She could stand on her back legs, raising her front legs up into the air, wearing a gauze tutu. She was a star attraction at Coney Island, and because of her fame she had her own trainer, a man named Gus, who fed her, bathed her, cleaned her stall, and naturally a bond was formed between them. Love, you could call it. Gus knew that love was essential in the training of animals and so he encouraged that love. He gave her bananas when she was good as a way to reinforce their affection. He also had a stick, which he used, but because for Topsy the connection they had was paramount, she loved him for the bananas and forgave him for the stick.

When she got older and her novelty wore off, Gus drifted away. Other, more important animals required his attention so that by 1900 she was mainly used for heavy labor. He hadn't exactly rejected her—he would still leave her some food—but he didn't bathe her, he didn't comfort her, and he certainly didn't return her love. That was what she wanted; that was what she was used to. When a person gets used to a thing and then that thing is taken away, the person becomes destabilized, and in that state it's not too hard to go a little crazy. Topsy didn't go crazy, but she was hurt and she was sad. And she couldn't talk about it. She didn't have the language.

She could think and feel, but she couldn't express herself because the language inside of her was elephant language, plus it was inside of her. And so, unable to communicate her thoughts and emotions, she started acting out. She was frustrated by her inability to affect her environment and so she became more difficult to work with. Elephants remember so well because their experiences are stored in their bodies, and they have big bodies, and her big body was filled with unpleasant thoughts and emotions. She tried to banish these thoughts and emotions but she couldn't. She couldn't deny them or ignore them because she was filled with them, literally.

One day after work two of Gus's friends stop by. They've been drinking and they're playing around, teasing Topsy, and one of them, as a joke, throws a lighted cigarette into her mouth. Because of the structure of the elephant mouth she can't spit it out; it continues to burn, like a fuse, until suddenly something explodes in her. From her face alone you wouldn't know. She looks calm and peaceful. From her big, sleepy eyes you wouldn't sense the rage, and she doesn't know her own rage, and when she turns, she's not aware of any particular desire to kill. She's not actually conscious of hating the two men, one of whom is standing against the main support post. But she grabs the man with her trunk, lifts him up, throws him against the post and there's nothing except the sound of the snapping of bones. A cry maybe, because Gus, who'd been outside, comes into the tent. The other man, the one who threw the cigarette, is on the ground underneath her foot, and partly out of anger, and partly out of her desire to communicate her unhappiness to Gus, she raises her foot over the man's face, and then she lets her foot come down.

First the man screams, and then the foot comes down. And then his head collapses, mixing in with the hay and the dung. Gus, over by the tent flap, is just watching, silhouetted against the light. The first man, still alive, limps away to the edge of the tent, and it wasn't just the cigarette, Topsy knows that. She watches Gus with her large eyes and she wants Gus to know what she's feeling. There's no recognition on his face but she's hoping. Even as she's surrounded by men with sharp poles she watches Gus to see if he knows what he's caused. As she is led away in chains she keeps looking back to see if now, finally, he understands.

There was a silent film made of Topsy's death. It was a one-minute short produced by Thomas Edison's manufacturing company. The camera was there, part of the semicircle of fifteen hundred spectators at the new Luna Park, on January 4. Topsy was standing, surrounded by people. The cameras started rolling. And then the six thousand volts of this new invention called electricity were sent into the elephant's body. At first nothing happened, then the quivering, then the throes. The smoke rising out of the bottom of her feet. The film captures the muscles of the elephant going limp and lifeless, the elephant remaining upright after the muscles had gone, and then the muscles stiffen, and then the huge beast collapses into the dust. The whole event took about ten seconds and the camera captured almost everything. The difference between the film version and actually being there is that in the film, when the elephant falls to the ground, there's silence. In 1903 at Luna Park the earth momentarily rumbled.

2. SAARTJIE, ALONE

The Hottentot Venus was the name given to an African woman who'd already been given the Afrikaans name Saartjie (*Sar*-key) Baartman. In 1810 she was brought from Cape Town, South Africa, to London, where she was exhibited as an oddity. She was a star attraction at the time. Not only was she African, she also had the physical characteristic known as steatopygia, an accumulation of fat on the buttocks, and it was her buttocks that were famous and became the focus of the show.

Crowds of people came and paid to see her walk, not quite naked, back and forth across a small stage. Sometimes she wore a gauze dress or a cape, but people didn't care about her clothes. They came to see her unusualness. She would turn around or bend over, depending on the requests from the spectators. And when she complied, as she always did, there were always the gasps of amazement and then a joke and then laughter. And at the beginning she didn't mind that much. Although the whole experience wasn't what she'd been promised back in Cape Town, she didn't want to quit. A world had opened up for her, and because she was intelligent she looked forward to learning about that world. She didn't enjoy the ridicule or the spit when people spat at her, but that was part of the world she was in, and she didn't want to leave that world. She just wanted to be happy in that world. She wanted the people to come to her show, but she wanted them to be different, to see her and treat her differently. And what she wanted didn't happen. And she couldn't talk about it. She couldn't say: "Will you please treat me with respect," or "Look at me as a person," or "Get rid of your prejudice." She spoke a little English but language wasn't the problem. The problem was the world she was in.

One night she was sleeping on her cot and she had to pee. So she had a dream, and in the dream she needed to go to the bathroom. She was desperately trying to find a bathroom, trying to negotiate through the world of the dream to a place where she could pee. She kept trying to find relief but not getting anywhere, and she wasn't getting anywhere because she wasn't searching in the right world. She was in the world of her dream, and in that world, even if she found a place to pee, it wouldn't have helped, because the world in which she really needed to pee was a different world. She needed to see that the dream world—which seemed completely real—was not the only world. She needed a bigger picture, one that included waking up and going to the bathroom.

When I said that language wasn't a problem, that wasn't quite right. As her novelty wore off the abuse increased, and her so-called negative emotions—her resentment and anger and fear—also increased. And she felt these things, but when she tried to express them she wasn't understood. These emotions stayed inside of her, and so, unable to communicate, and unable to see any way she *could* communicate, she began acting out; she became difficult to work with. Frustrated by her inability to affect the world she was living in, she began hating that world.

In 1814 she was sold or traded to a traveling circus and taken to Paris. She had her ups and downs and she died a year later at the age of twenty-six. She was never considered totally and completely human by the people who observed her, and except for her genitals we don't know what she looked like. Scientists at the time, trying to prove some then-current theory about racial characteristics, dissected her and removed her genitals and her brain from her body.

These were then placed in jars and put on display in Paris, at the Museum of Man.

3. GANESHA, THE STORY

Ganesha is a kind of elephant, and he's also a god in India. He has an elephant head and a human body, and he's usually shown riding a rat or a mouse. He is the god of wisdom, the god of obstacles and the remover of obstacles, and because he's a mythical figure, the story of how he got his elephant head has many variations.

In one version his mother, Parvati, is taking a bath. She wants privacy and so she tells Ganesha to guard the door. Shiva, his father, comes to the house in disguise and when Ganesha refuses to let him enter, Shiva cuts his head off. When his mother finds out, she's so disconsolate that Shiva transplants onto the young man's body the head of a passing elephant.

In another version, my version, Ganesha is a young man and being a mythical figure he's been given a test. There's always a mythical test and this particular test is to go to the edge of the known world. There's a river there and he's told to cross that river.

Before he goes his mother warns him not to be fooled by demons. And by demons she means his so-called negative emotions, his hatred and resentment. He's reminded not to see these emotions as anything other than passing. Thoughts and emotions come, he is told. And then they go. Neither grasp them nor push them away.

So, with this in mind, he sets out. He walks, day after day, until he comes to the end of the known world and there, just as he was told, is a river, although it's more like a stream. But it is a river. A man with a small boat is sitting on a rock near the edge of the river. Ganesha could easily have crossed the river on foot without a boat, but the boat was idle and he wanted to talk to the man. He walked to where the man was sitting, wrapped in scarves, his legs brown from the river mud. He says to the man something like "May I rent your boat?" or "Will you ferry me across the stream?" or "What's the cost to cross over?" But the man doesn't speak. In fact the man doesn't acknowledge Ganesha's existence.

Ganesha tries to get his attention but the man is absolutely still. He's not deaf; he's just not responding, and Ganesha would like some response. He tries to communicate with the man, and not just by speaking; he signals to the man and even touches the man but somehow he can't get through. He speaks again, carefully explaining his situation and why the boat would be helpful, and also casually mentioning that his father is the greatest god in the Hindu patheon. But the man takes no notice. Ganesha keeps trying to connect, stubbornly repeating his needs, getting more adamant about the boat. The boat, he says. And just as stubbornly the man remains impassive.

And at that moment a bird passes between him and the sun and for a flash he's in shadow. Something changes. He hears a voice; it's the voice of his mother. He looks down into the stream and a small, round pebble in the stream is talking to him, reminding him not to be fooled by his own impulses, not to believe that what he feels is anything other than what it is, feeling. And Ganesha knows that. He knows his emotions are transient and he knows he could let them go and let the man go and just walk across the river to the other world. But he finds himself fearful of leaving the world he knows; he's drawn to that world, and to the man, and to his struggle with the man, even though he's frustrated by the man's incomprehension. He's offended, in fact, by the man's insensitivity and lack of common courtesy. The man is being unreasonable.

And Ganesha is at a kind of fork in his path. He could have listened to the pebble, seen his emotions for what they were, and let them go. But Ganesha can't hear the pebble anymore because his anger and resentment are boiling up and these feelings seem absolutely real to him. He has to do something. So he approaches the man, to teach him a lesson. He faces the man. He plants his feet on the ground, raises his fists into the air, and that's when the man—Shiva in disguise—stands, and cuts Ganesha's head off. At that moment, not too far away, an elephant is about to die.

4. HOTTENTOT, IN LOVE

Paris, it's been said, is the city of lovers, and while she was living there, sure enough, Saartjie fell in love. She didn't come into contact, real contact, with that many people so naturally the person she fell in love with was her keeper, the man who fed her and led her to the stage where she made her money. As a whim the man encouraged her love. It was also his money she was making, and to that extent he cared about her happiness. Mainly he wanted the novelty, the proximity to fame, and of course the affection. They shared a kind of affection.

The thing about sex is that, at least for an instant, it's real. And in her mind that reality expanded. She took that sliver of love and expanded it, believed in it, and let it make her happy, even if the actual love she received was usually abusive. She forgave him that because she wanted to preserve the possibility of happiness. Saartjie was trying to satisfy her need for human connection in the only way she knew, by loving. And here was a possibility, a man who did more than just look. He talked to her, sometimes, and when he felt like it he touched her. He was, in her world, about as good as it got. Although he wasn't that good. He certainly didn't care for her. And she realized that the love she'd been creating was an illusion, and she knew that happiness meant waking up. But to what? The world she lived in was the only world she knew. She didn't know there *was* another world.

One night she was invited to a high-society ball, a fancy costume party where her unusualness would be the conversation piece. The man escorted her about as far as the front door and then disappeared into the crowd. She looked around. There were rooms of people and paintings painted on walls. Statues were everywhere and the stairways were carved and polished. People were dressed as soldiers and queens, and some of them wore masks. Saartjie didn't have a mask but her costume was excellent. She was a bird. She'd spent the prior week sewing pink feathers to what we now call a bikini, although at the time the concept of bikini didn't exist. But she had her outfit. And she wore a pair of shiny silver slippers. She walked down the marble steps into the grand salon. A woman with a long gown and white, creamy skin began talking to her and she began talking to the woman. Although her French was only rudimentary they carried on an intense and wide-ranging conversation. They stood next to a fountain with water bubbling and the woman treated her as if she was a human being. Men approached her and asked her to dance and food was brought to her on trays of silver. She thought she was in another world. In her effort to take in every aspect of this world— speaking with the woman, drinking champagne from a crystal glass—she'd completely forgotten about the man.

Well, not completely. She wasn't 100 percent focused on the party because about 1 percent of her was thinking about the man. He'd gotten into her thoughts and maybe about 5 percent was thinking about him, but she was looking at the people dancing and hearing the music and roughly 20 percent of her mind was on the man and she was looking at the woman, trying to listen to the woman but she was thinking about the man, so much so that the conversation ended and the woman walked away. Now it was only the man, and she wanted to be free of him. She wanted *not* to turn and begin looking across the room to find his face. She wanted to wake up. She realized that the man would probably hurt her, but she was more and more forgetting what that hurt was like. She felt the impulse pulling her, like a string rooted to her heart, and there was something that she needed, she felt it. He was cold and calm and terrible and yet she turned. She swirled around to find the thing that gave her, really, very little happiness.

5 . ELEPHANT, DYING

The day Topsy died was a cold, cold day, which didn't stop the people from coming out to watch. Electricity was a novelty and movies were a novelty, but death was the main attraction. Topsy had been tied with chains and ropes, not because she was a man-killer, but because man-killers made publicity and publicity drew crowds. And they were there, gathered in a semicircle, with the ocean behind them, facing an area cleared of rubble. Luna Park was still under construction and so an area was cleared where Topsy was going to die. And she knew she was going to die. That's why she was uncooperative during the slow procession through the mud. They had a little trouble getting her out of her stall and they wanted Gus to help but he wouldn't do it; even when they offered him twenty-five dollars he still refused. But he watched when they led her onto the makeshift stage. Her feet were guided onto thin wooden slippers, pieces of wood attached to her feet that would contain the electric current and keep it from passing through the ground into the innocent spectators. Thick ropes held her in place so that when she fell she wouldn't fall far. And then they attached the electrodes—one to her right front foot and one to her left rear.

Topsy was facing the crowd, looking at them, and of course she was thinking of Gus. Unlike Saartjie, who wanted *not* to want her keeper, Topsy didn't care. She was tired of trying to be free of Gus and the habit of Gus and now she'd given up; it was too much trouble. Plus she was going to die. If there was ever a time she needed comfort or what passed for comfort, this was it. That's why she was scanning the crowd to find his face, that familiar thing she was counting on to take her away from where she was. She wasn't feeling that great and she was craving a little Gus, just a shot. Just a sliver. She saw women, and children eating candy, and men in caps, but not Gus. She kept looking for Gus, worried now and desperate. No more struggling for a happiness that seemed to be always eluding her. She wasn't interested in happiness anymore. She just wanted Gus. If she'd had a voice she would have called out.

And then she saw him. There he was in his clean white shirt and his old, familiar cap. She looked into his face and waited for something to happen, she didn't care what it was—comfort, disappointment—it didn't matter. She wanted from Gus what she'd always wanted, a connection, even a failed connection, and she stood there, waiting, but it wasn't happening. She could feel the cold metal of the electrodes digging into her skin. And his eyes; they weren't exactly vacant but they weren't doing anything. She kept looking at them, hoping something would happen, expecting it to happen. And when it didn't, she looked at the other people, at the men and women staring at her, and they all looked the same to her, they all looked human. In their own eyes they might have seen a thousand subtle differences, but to Topsy they were indistinguishable. She was looking at them, and then beyond them, slightly, over their heads, to the ocean. She could see the waves forming and reforming in lines along the water. She was looking at the waves in the cold, calm sea.

And then the current entered her body. The sea got darker. She was watching it get darker and darker, and she opened her eyes and reached out through her eyes, watching the waves fade, one after the other, until finally they disappeared completely.

THE JUDGMENT
OF PSYCHO

1

— You eat like a bird.
— You'd know, of course.

Janet Leigh was never completely naked during the filming of Alfred Hitchcock's *Psycho*, but she did have breasts. They're hinted at and alluded to, never revealed exactly, but she did have them, and in a way it's why she was killed. The movie begins with her, with a long shot of Phoenix, Arizona. The camera pans across the city to a building, to a window in the building, then under the venetian blinds of the window and into the room where Janet Leigh is lying half-naked on a bed. She's wearing a white bra and a white slip, and the bra, sitting on top of her chest like two white pyramids, looks as if it ought to be enough protection.

A man is standing over her. His name is Sam, her lover. She's just had sex with Sam so everything at this point ought to be glowing, but it isn't. Janet Leigh is in love with Sam but Sam keeps talking about his problem. He says he has a problem—he calls it a money problem—which precludes him from getting married and he suggests, if she wants to get married, that she find someone else, someone more available. But she doesn't want someone else, and later, when an opportunity at work presents itself, she steals a lot of money, buys a car, and drives to California, where Sam works in a hardware store.

She drives all day and during the night it starts raining, and her wipers don't work, and the rain makes it hard to see, and the headlights shine in her eyes, and so, confused and disoriented, she finds herself on a small, deserted road. It's suddenly quiet. She pulls off the road into the parking lot of the Bates Motel, where Anthony Perkins plays the part of the innkeeper. He's long-necked, broad-shouldered, and because he's a psycho he seems quite nice. He gives her the key to room number one and while he's showing her the room they make a little date, for supper.

As he runs up to the old Victorian house on the hill to prepare the sandwiches, Tony Perkins doesn't want to seem too happy or too buoyant; he doesn't want to have desires because he doesn't want his mother taking them away.

We can hear from far away the voices coming from the house.

"What are you so happy about, Boy?"

"Nothing, Mother."

"Don't nothing me, Boy. I know who's down there."

"She's lost, Mother."

"And you're the one who'll show her the way? What do you know about the way, Boy?"

The voice is threatening when it says, "She'll not be appeasing her ugly appetites with my food, or my son." And when the voice says, "I refuse to speak of disgusting things," it's referring to desire. And since Tony Perkins is filled with desire he leaves the house, bringing the tray of butter and sliced bread down to the motel veranda where he and Janet Leigh go into the . . . They almost go into the bedroom but Tony has trouble with "bedroom," with saying the word, so they go instead into the parlor, next door, where "it's nicer," he says, "and warmer."

And they sit.

His hobby is taxidermy and the walls of the parlor are stuffed with examples of his handiwork. He doesn't like the look of "beasts," he says, so the walls are filled with birds. Janet Leigh looks around at the eyes staring down at her.

"It's a strange hobby," she says. "Curious."

"And not as expensive as you'd think," he says. As he fondles one of his glass-eyed birds he says, "It's more than just a hobby." He's not shy talking about his birds, or about his mother. "Sometimes," he says, "I want to go up there and curse her and leave her forever, or at least defy her. But I know I can't." He also says, referring to his mother, "A son is a poor substitute for a lover," and this is when it dawns on Janet Leigh that Tony might be slightly mad. He's nervous and fidgety, constantly sucking on pieces of candy; but he's also lucid. "We're all in our private traps," he says. "We scratch and claw, but only at the air, only at each other." And in talking to him she realizes that she has stepped into her own kind of trap, and she decides then to return to Phoenix, to take the money back and face her life.

As an audience we half hope these two attractive young people might come together, help each other, and find a little happiness. But Hitchcock doesn't let that happen. Janet Leigh, although she's somewhat flirtatious, isn't really interested in Tony Perkins and his awkward solicitations. She has other things on her mind and basically she rejects him. Tony Perkins, for his part, is watching the woman sitting across from him, chewing bites of buttered bread, not looking at her breasts. He's making a special effort *not* to look at the area that fascinates him the most. He's beginning to feel things that are exciting and frightening. Something is happening to him, he knows that, but he doesn't know exactly what it is.

2

The Trojan War begins like this: A young man named Paris is resting on his elbow in a lush green meadow filled with trees and grass and there's a stream flowing through the middle of this paradise. Three goddesses are standing in front of him—Hera, Athena, and Aphrodite. They're posing, waiting to be chosen by this young man, and to that end they've offered him gifts. Hera, queen of the gods, has offered him power. Athena, the goddess of war, has offered him victory in battle. Aphrodite, the goddess of beauty and love, has promised him the most beautiful woman in the world. Which is what he wants: Helen. The most beautiful woman in the world. With Aphrodite's help he goes to her, woos her, and seduces her away from her husband, the king, and carries her back to Troy.

Paris doesn't know the ramifications of his actions because he doesn't want to know. He chose Helen not because he needed her but because she inspired in him more desire. He was living on a beautiful mountaintop with a beautiful woman and yet he couldn't resist the possibility of having something more, of choosing a new kind of luxury. He was excited by the temptation of picking either A or B or C, and he didn't realize it was a multiple-choice question. He could have picked "none of the above." He could have said, "No thanks. I appreciate the opportunity but I'm fine here on my mountaintop with the woman who loves me." He could have seen the story in a completely different light. But then he wouldn't have been Paris.

The Judgment of Paris is a painting by Lucas Cranach, and in the painting the goddesses are completely naked. Aphrodite has a thin veil covering part of her body but basically they're naked. Paris is fully clothed. It's his judgment, and because they're naked, even though they're goddesses, they're his women. They're his women, but only in a dream. In the painting he's shown with his eyes turned dreamily upward, and in the story the goddesses have been brought to him in a dream. But he doesn't know that. He thinks they're real. He believes they actually are standing in front of him, naked and completely exposed. And to the extent that it's a dream, they are. But it's not *just* a dream. When he chooses one particular goddess, the other two feel rejected, naturally, and they hate that. It kills them to be rejected, and when something kills a goddess, something else has to die.

3

—*If you love someone you don't do that to them, even if you hate them.*

I'm surprised Tony Perkins didn't say to Janet Leigh, "We're closed, ma'am," and tell her to go back home. By the time he gave her the key to room number one it was probably too late. He probably knew then what was going to happen. Like the Trojans. They left the young Paris to die on the top of a craggy mountain because of a warning that he would cause the destruction of their city, and although they tried to alter the course of events, he caused the destruction of their city.

When Janet Leigh finishes her bread and butter, Tony doesn't want her to leave; he wants her to stay and talk. Here is an attractive woman with delicate skin sitting in his parlor speaking to him as if he actually is a normal human man. This is amazing to him, and suddenly he's in love. He doesn't know what that means exactly, but he feels it, and he feels he's in it, and it might've been beautiful too except the next scene is the peephole scene.

Janet Leigh goes back to her room. Tony stands facing the camera, and Hitchcock lights him from the side so that half his face is brightly lit and half his face is in darkness. He swallows, listening to the footsteps receding, to the door opening next door, and that's when he walks over to the painting on the wall, lifts it off its nail and sets it on the floor. We see the small peephole notched in the wall and we see Tony looking in the peephole and we see Janet Leigh taking off her clothes. This time she's wearing a black bra and a black slip, and when the film cuts back to Tony's eye, watching, we can only imagine what he sees. All we know is that he's overcome.

Desire has been roused in him. This beautiful creature has released in him a lifetime of repressed desire, hidden until now, like Janet Leigh's breasts have been hidden, beneath the bra, beneath the sweater, and he doesn't want to look at them. But he *does* want to look at them. She's standing in front of him, completely naked, teasing and taunting, and the young man who lives with his mother is coaxed and tortured into feelings he cannot have. He has them but he cannot have them, therefore something has to change, and the thing that changes is the young man himself. The injunction is there; he can not—absolutely not—experience desire because it goes against the wishes of his mother, his dead mother whose voice is clear and strong and vindictive, and so he denies the person who has the desire: himself. When he feels desire coming up, or anything inside of him coming up, he automatically denies its existence. He denies it because he hates it; he hates it because it's painful; it's painful because it frightens him; it frightens him because it's forbidden; it's forbidden because it threatens his mother. And when something threatens her, something has to die.

But he doesn't want to think about that. He's spent a lifetime not thinking about that or feeling that, and as he watches Janet Leigh the feelings she inspires in him and the struggle she creates in him become unbearable. That's when he runs out of the parlor and up the steps to the old house. We see him hesitate at the foot of the staircase, then walk down the hallway to the kitchen where he sits in his chair at the table, rocking and listening. Listening to his own voice which is silent, and his mother's voice which he hates, deciding what he should do, or be.

4

When it comes to influence the old masters are almost never wrong. I'm thinking about the kind of influence that isn't seen or known but is always there. In the painting by the Dutch painter Jan Vermeer called *Girl Asleep at a Table*, we see a girl. She's sitting at a table, her eyes closed. She's doing something. She's dreaming. Or she's thinking. Of love? Or her future? Or what happened in her past? I'm asking these questions but we already know the answers because scientists have taken radiographic pictures of this painting and standing next to the woman, behind the pigment, covered over with paint, there's a man. We know he's there, standing slightly to her left, in the doorway. He's standing there and she doesn't even know it. And because she doesn't know he's there his influence is even more pervasive. She goes out to walk along the street, along the cobblestones in her little Dutch shoes, shopping at the cheese store, picking out some Edam cheese or some Gouda cheese and there she is, weighing in her mind what to buy, and every decision she makes is influenced by this man standing over her shoulder. He's a shadow following her and she can't escape. She goes back to the house and sits at the table and I almost want to change the title of the painting. I want to call it *Woman Who Is Influenced by the Man Standing in the Doorway Without Knowing He's There.* Or *Man Standing in a Doorway Influencing a Woman Who Doesn't Know He Even Exists.* Or *Woman Who Is Frightened.* Yes, I think she's frightened because she senses a presence. She wants to shake off this unknown influence and get on with her life, and yet the man is there, painted over but he's there, and so she's frightened, and she doesn't want to be frightened. She can get on with her life if she's not frightened, and the way she's not frightened is to not be aware. And because she's not aware of him, this man, or this ghost, continues to haunt her, standing beside her throughout her life.

—*I don't mind.*
—*But you should mind.*
—*Oh I do. But I say I don't.*

When we destroy ourselves we probably know what we're doing, and yet at the same time, for the destruction to proceed without resistance, we have to be unaware. Tony Perkins knows his mother is an apparition, and yet at the same time he believes she's absolutely real. As an audience we only see his mother through shower curtains and window shades; we can easily guess that she might be a figment of his mind. But she's the one who parts the shower curtain and stabs Janet Leigh over and over, and so she's not just an apparition. Especially not to Tony. She's real to him, and powerful, and she's taken over. He hates her but "A boy's best friend is his mother," he says. "She needs me," he says, but really it's the other way around. He needs the apparition. Without it he'd be lost.

Which is why he lets himself be pulled up the thick wooden staircase into his mother's corner room where he paces back and forth, inhaling the smell of the room's decay, listening to the voice that bids him to go to the dark armoire and open it. Which he does. He takes out the shoe box with the wig inside and lays it on the bed. He lays all her things on the bed and then he lays himself beside them. He adjusts himself on the bed to follow the contours of her indentation. In this way he can finally relax; he can finally let go of the tension that's killing him.

He can sleep the sleep of the passive. And in that sleep of passivity his mother can now wake up.

And she does. She rolls over, swings her legs off the bed, onto the floor, and stands. She takes the ragged dress and, as if in a trance, gathers it, lifting her arms and letting the long, motherly material fall over her head. She straightens the hem, looks at herself in the mirror, adjusts the collar, the cuffs, and then she takes the top off the shoe box. By the time she pulls her hair back and sets the gray elastic cap tight around her skull, Tony's completely gone. It's not him sweating in the mirror; it's excitement, and excitement covers up a lot. She doesn't know what she's doing because she doesn't want to know.

She finds herself in the kitchen, where the knives are kept, and she opens the drawer and selects a long and shiny one. She wants to kill. Filled with the rage her son refuses to feel, she wants to swoop down like a bird of prey and kill the thing that's causing his disturbance. She knows she's dead but she can't, or won't, admit it. Her fingernails are still growing, she can see that. Her fingers are holding the knife. And yet she's not holding it. She's not herself today. She's gone today. Gone beyond. And yet she keeps floating back, like the bodies in the pond, bubbling up, and as she flies out of the house, down the steps to room number one, she knows it's a—not a trick, but yes, in a way. It's her trick, and yet she's the one who's confused by it, and lost in it, and caught in the sleight of mind that turns her again and again into something she doesn't want to be. But she believes it's the only way. She wants to do something different, to stop the repetition, but she believes she has no choice. The thing she hates is the thing she embraces, over and over and over. That's why they call the movie *Psycho*.

6

Hector knows he's going to die. He remembers the prophesy foretelling his death and he knows that there's nothing he can do. During the long siege of Troy it becomes clear that Paris is neither a leader nor a fighter. He isn't even a lover, so Athena turns her attention to his brother, Hector, the commander of the Trojan forces, and she aims her fury at him. Specifically what she aims at him is Achilles, the greatest of the Argive warriors. With his powerful arms and godlike shield he's practically invincible. He has Athena's anger on his side, and he also has his own, which makes him immune to fear. Hector, in contrast, is a family man, a Tamer of Horses; he loves his wife and his children, and although he's a general, he's frightened.

As are his parents. Watching from the wall of the city, his father is pulling his hair out, beseeching his son to come inside the wall to safety. His mother, in that more emotive time, has actually pulled aside her dress, and cupping her breast in her hand, offers it to her son, as if he could go back to the safety of his childhood.

But Hector is firm. He's firm and he's also ambivalent. He doesn't want to die, but he doesn't want to be a coward. But he's not a fool, so when Achilles lifts his spear to fight, Hector starts running. And Achilles follows. Around and around the city they run, three times, and they would probably run forever, like figures on a Grecian urn, except that the gods are not impartial. Zeus lets Athena loose and suddenly Hector's brother, his favorite brother, is standing next to him on the open plain. When Hector sees his brother he thinks that help has come. His brother is willing to risk his life and when the brother says, "I'm with you," Hector's heart is filled with hope. And yes, he remembers the prophesy, but now he's not alone. His own brother is supporting him, and when your own brother appears like that, maybe the gods have changed their minds. Thinking this, he stops running and faces Achilles.

Achilles lifts his spear, and this is when Hector steps forward and attempts to negotiate, to arrange that whoever dies will receive a decent burial. But Achilles doesn't get it. Achilles has been holding this terrible rage in his chest, waiting for this moment to finally be free, and so there's no discussion. Achilles lifts his great spear and sets it sailing at the Trojan, who watches it fly through the air and, because he sees it clearly, at the last minute, he moves out of its way. Then Hector, who is an excellent shot, aims his own spear at the great Greek warrior and with the whole of his strength sends it flying to its target. But Achilles has a shield made by gods and easily deflects the spear. He's looking straight at Hector, and suddenly he's holding his spear in his hand again. Hector needs a spear and so he turns to his brother.

And that's when he understands that the world he was seeing was not the world he was living in, that what he'd based his life on was a trick, an apparition. And he looks up and standing next to Achilles, hovering slightly above him, radiant, glowing, and smiling, is the owl-eyed virgin, Athena, the goddess who hates him. Hector sees his death. He sees there is no brother standing with him, and never was, and at that moment his stomach falls away. The story has Hector pleading again but I think the story's wrong. What happened was this: Achilles lifts his spear and says, "Get down on your knees, you Trojan dog, and pray for my pity," and Hector says, "No." He says, "I've had enough of you. Get out of my city. Get out of my land. Take your violence and your war and your hatred and leave forever." Achilles then heaves his spear. It finds the point at the collarbone where the plates of Hector's armor come together. It pierces Hector's flesh, and he dies.

—We all go a little mad sometimes.

The woman with the large hands and the cheap wig walks out of the house on the hill. Although it's not raining she holds with her hand the hem of her dress off the ground; with her other hand she holds the knife. Her boots are heavy walking down the steps and across the veranda. At room number one the door is unlocked and she steps inside. She can smell the soap and fresh shampoo drifting out from underneath the bathroom door. She can't hear the noise of the shower because her head is filled with the noise of her thinking, a thinking she acts upon as she opens the bathroom door, steps up to the semitransparent curtain.

She can't hear the sound of the curtain parting.

She can't hear the sound of stabbing.

She can't see the water in the drain turning red because she's running back to the house, through the heavy door, up the thick stairs, and into the room.

Her son, hearing her heavy boots, is just waking up. "Mother," he says. "Oh god, Mother. Blood, blood."

She's holding the knife in the position of stabbing, dumb and expressionless. Tony stands up to her, reaches to take the knife, or try to, but she doesn't give it up. Blood is dripping off its tip and he's got his fingers around her wrists trying to pull the fingers off and loosen the grip but she's strong. She's old but she's strong, and they struggle. He throws her down on the bed, falling on top of her, pinning her hands above her head, screaming into her face, telling her unblinking eyes that it's over, that it has to be over. But it's not over for him. He hates her power and so he keeps wrestling with that power. And her body. He's pressing himself into the body, writhing and fighting with the body of this ghost, struggling with a ghost who might as well be dead.

THE FACES OF
JOAN OF ARC

1. TRYING TO BE

Mercedes McCambridge plays the role of the devil in a movie called *The Exorcist*. She's never actually seen in the movie because the devil is difficult to see, but as the *voice* of the devil she's entered the realm of the human. She's taken over the body of a young girl in an effort to live her life and the only problem is: for her to live that life, the girl has to die.

In the movie the girl is tied to a bed, and coming out from inside of her is the voice of the devil saying things like "Fuck me, fuck me" to the two priests. The devil just wants to be left alone so it can do whatever work it feels it has to do and here are these men with their vials of "holy water" trying to burn the devil out. The water is bitter, and it stings, and the devil thinks, "They're trying to get rid of me." Naturally the devil fights back.

Mercedes McCambridge fought what was called a drinking problem. She didn't work for a while because of alcohol abuse, and while she lay in the sweat-stained bed of the rehabilitation hospital her doctors told her to love herself.

"Love yourself," they said. "Accept yourself." They were saying "Love yourself," but what they were doing, or how they were acting, was saying something else. They were telling her to choose *certain* parts of herself, urging her to love *these* parts, and this was confusing. Because the choices they gave her were not all the choices.

In the movie the men were repulsed by the devil and the stench of the devil; they told the devil to leave the girl and to cease to exist. And of course the devil couldn't do that. The devil had come into this girl for a reason and it wasn't going to leave. Mercedes McCambridge, in the hospital, was listening to the doctors telling her to love certain parts of herself and hate other parts of herself and so she tried; she began hating the part that drank Jim Beam—the whiskey. But still she drank it. And the more she did, the more she hated that part of herself, and the more she hated it, the more she focused on, and identified with, the thing she hated, until at some point she started hating herself.

2. TORTURE

Joan of Arc, the actual person, was born in 1412 and burned at the stake in 1431. That makes her about nineteen years old when she was put on trial for living her life. That's all she was trying to do. She felt she knew the reason she was put on earth, and when she started pursuing that reason, the authorities felt threatened. She wore the clothes of a man, and although this bothered them slightly, what really bothered them was her insistence that she could communicate with god. That was *their* job and that's why they had her arrested.

In Carl Dreyer's silent movie *The Passion of Joan of Arc*, the role of Joan was played by a woman named Renée Falconetti, and although she wasn't burned at the stake she felt, or imagined that she felt, or wanted to feel, what it felt to be Joan of Arc. This was the only film she ever made and because she sought this identification she cut her hair short like Joan's hair, and she wore, like Joan, the clothes of a man. It wasn't that she wanted the *look* that Joan had; what she wanted was the *authority* Joan had, over her own life.

In the story, the judges want her to sign a statement denying that she hears the voice of god, or that she speaks with angels, or that her life has a mission. At first, because she *does* hear voices, she refuses to sign. But later, when she's threatened with torture, she reluctantly signs the paper, and this is what Falconetti can't quite understand. She relates to the saint in Joan but not to the nineteen-year-old girl, and that's why, one day, after everyone else has left the set, she stands in the middle of the specially built dungeon, looking at the light stands and scaffolding, and also the instruments of torture. She sees a metal plate—about as tall as she is—leaning against the wall, covered with spikes, and she walks to this plate and she touches one of the spikes. She presses her finger against the point, letting her finger, and the sensitive nerves beneath the ridges of her fingertip, find the pain in the spike. Joan of Arc would never betray herself for a little pain, she thinks, and she takes the edges of the plate, pulls it away from the wall, and then she lies down on her back on the tiled floor. And as she does she pulls the plate on top of her. She's wearing a light cotton dress and at first the plate doesn't hurt. It lies on her like a lover, on her hip bones and rib cage, and the spikes aren't sharp enough to penetrate into her body, and although it's heavy, it's not *that* heavy, and she lets her hands, which had been holding the plate, go limp, and it feels good, in a strange way, but as she relaxes and lets the weight of it sink into her flesh it starts to feel less good, and then less good, and then it starts to hurt, and she thinks that if she can accept it, the pain might go away, and she tries, and although the pain does go away, it comes right back, worse than before, and she wants to accept it but finally she can't, and she screams out. She screams, and then she pushes the plate off her body. And the next day, for the scene when she has to submit to the judges, she does. The withered old men assure her that it is her choice, that the decision to sign the paper is up to *her*, but really what choice does she have? If she doesn't agree she knows what will happen. She remembers the spikes pressing into her skin and she's willing to do what they want. She's willing to say that her work is the work of the devil.

3 . OBEDIENCE

Hedy Lamarr plays Delilah in the movie *Samson and Delilah*, and yes, she cuts off the hair of Victor Mature. Samson is played by Victor Mature and although she loves him, when the king requires someone to destroy this seemingly indestructible man she makes a decision. Actually the decision is made earlier, when she feels rejected by Victor Mature. That's the point at which she gives herself a choice: either experience the pain of the rejection or avoid the pain and do something else—anything else—and because that pain, to her, is a kind of torture, she turns against it. She turns against the thing she loves and responds to her king's command by obediently and ambitiously seducing Victor Mature. When she has him sleeping, finally, with his powerful head in her lap, she clips off the source of his power—his hair—so that he can then be blinded.

In 1932, when she was about nineteen years old, Hedy Lamarr made the film for which she became famous—*Extase*. The reason it was famous, or the reason she was famous in it, was because of a brief scene that showed her scampering naked through a primeval forest. By the time she arrived in Hollywood, partly because of that scene, she was considered the most beautiful woman in the world and when people saw her, what they saw was her beauty. Because people looked at her as if she were a painting or a statue, she took on the attributes of a painting or a statue, and she began to build herself a wall. If people didn't know her, when they saw her, what they saw was this wall of beauty. She hated the wall because she couldn't get over it, into the world, but also she loved the wall because it was comfortable and reassuring and safe. And also because she'd built it.

One reason she was attracted to Samson was because when he looked at her he saw beyond the wall, past the beauty that protected her. And because of this you might think that when she made the choice to betray Victor Mature she might've had some questions or some doubts, and maybe she did. But she never questioned the assumption of the choice itself. She accepted that her decision was between either A or B, that those were the choices. And because choice number A was intolerable she turned from what she knew to be reality—her pain—hoping that somehow her decision would lead to some abeyance of that pain, and therefore to happiness. She didn't want to see that the choice itself was flawed, that in denying what she hated she was also denying the other thing, her love, and so what she created was the opposite of happiness. She followed a path leading away from where she wanted to go until, at the end of the movie, in a moment of realization, she redeems herself, partially, by causing the destruction of her city. In the movie, Hedy Lamarr helps Victor Mature pull down the walls of the temple. In her actual *life*, however, it wasn't that easy.

4 . CYNICISM

Hedy Lamarr, through most of the movie, takes the side of those in authority, which is not the same as *having* authority. Obedience is a way of reconciling oneself to a lack of authority or a lack of choice. But it's not the only way.

Anna Karina was a Danish model who moved to France in 1958 and began making movies with Jean-Luc Godard when she was about nineteen years old. In the first movie they made together she played an undercover soldier fighting for a noble cause and during the filming they fell in love. They were married in 1961 and continued making movies, and because he was a director and she was an actor he decided what parts she would play. In their next film she played a girl who sleeps with her husband's friend, and in the films after that she started playing prostitutes. *Vivre Sa Vie* begins with her looking for some meaning in her life. She doesn't have a clear idea of how she wants to live until she meets a bon vivant who offers her what seems to be a choice. She can continue to live a life that seems empty or she can become a prostitute and make a lot of money. Because she's part of the modern world she needs a lot of money, or feels she needs a lot of money, and so the choice seems reasonable. Actually it doesn't seem that reasonable, but she learns the trick of not noticing. She develops the ability not to care, which is cynicism. Although her mind keeps returning to what she thought was her empty life she forces herself to practice her trade, and as she gets better and better, she divorces herself more and more from her actions. She creates a space between what she does and who she feels she is, so at least she can live with a little peace. She tells herself it doesn't matter what she does, that what matters is her happiness. And we all want to find some happiness, and that's why she starts looking for whatever scraps she can find. It's why she starts shopping. It makes her happy, briefly, to have some power over merchandise.

5 . THE DEVIL'S DILEMMA

Mercedes McCambridge felt the spikes pressing into her body. Not exactly spikes because there were no spikes, but she felt something and it was painful and she called it hatred. She hated herself. And when she did, what she usually did was reach for a bottle. As she poured the whiskey into the glass she felt disgust for herself, and to disguise that feeling or distract that feeling, or frighten it away, she said, "I am the devil."

When she agreed to play in the movie *Touch of Evil,* the director, Orson Welles, told her she needed a haircut. "Okay," she said. "Fine." She wasn't vain, and she sat in a folding chair and let him stand behind her, but Orson Welles, instead of cutting anything, coated her hair with black grease and sculpted the boyish hairdo she would have for the scene in which a young bride is terrorized. In the scene, she was supposed to portray something evil. He told her, basically, "You are the devil."

And it's not that the devil is incapable of love. It's just that what the devil calls "love," we call "evil," and we try to eradicate that evil. In *The Exorcist* they've tied the girl down and with their water and curses and crosses they're trying to destroy a thing that just wants some kind of existence. But they don't give the devil a choice. And the devil, naturally, is upset. It's hard to think of the devil being scared but that's why it spits out the thick green bile. To sicken the priests. To drive them away. And they *are* sickened. The old priest has a heart attack, the young priest starts hallucinating, and let's say that Mercedes McCambridge is the devil. She needs the body of the girl to survive. Without the body of the girl she doesn't exist, so she says, "Don't take me away from the girl," or "Don't take the girl away from me," but the director of the movie doesn't give her that choice. Sitting under the fleshy arms of Orson Welles she doesn't have a choice. Sitting at her kitchen table, alone, feeling the hatred rising in her body, she doesn't give her*self* a choice because she can't see any choice, and her response to that lack of choice is to drink. And when she drinks, sure enough, she's unhappy. And we would hope at least that if she's not going to be happy, then the devil in her might be happy. But no. The devil will never be happy because the devil isn't given any choice.

6. UNHAPPINESS

Hedy Lamarr had just about given up on happiness. But not quite. She'd gone to the large department store on Wilshire Boulevard because she was looking for the happiness that was always eluding her. As she walked across the tiled floor she wasn't aware that her heart was beating a little faster than normal. Or that a thin layer of moisture had formed at the small of her back and between her breasts.

Walking down the aisles of this department store, Hedy Lamarr is no longer the most beautiful woman in the world, but when a salesgirl shows her a long, flowing coat she's reminded of the time when she was. And the coat, she knows, is only a coat, but when she tries it on and looks in the mirror she imagines what people will see. She dreams that people will see her as beautiful. And not just beauty. When she says something funny she imagines that people will laugh and say, "She cracks me up," or "You crack me up." And then suddenly she takes off the coat and moves to another rack where she sees a dress, a red dress, and although her mind keeps returning to the coat she forces herself to take the red dress and hold it up. She thinks to herself how gaudy it is, and how stupid. It's red, but it's cheap, not sexy. And yet she takes it into the dressing room, sits down, and in the privacy of the carpeted cubicle she looks at her face in the mirror, at the lines at the sides of her eyes, at the mole on her neck. You should look as good as you feel, she thinks, and she tries to feel something. She's barely aware of the odor of nervousness coming out of her, like the scent of a zealot, or someone insane. She takes off her sweater and skirt, puts on the red dress, and zips the zipper. She tugs it up so it fits her chest and she doesn't look at herself in the mirror. She puts her own skirt on over the dress, and she puts her sweater on over the dress, and when she walks out of the cubicle into the store she tries to look as normal as possible. Like the mannequins and salespeople around her. When she looks outside she can see through the doors of the store to the people outside, and the sky which is blue and boundless. She turns toward the door and as she walks to the door a girl, a tall girl with black hair, says to her, "This is you," and sprays her with some perfume. Music is coming from somewhere in the store and as she turns and follows the sound she watches the feet in her shoes as they hit the tiled floor. When some hair falls in her face she places it behind her ear. A bead of sweat rolls down the inside of her arm and she thinks, I'm staining the dress. She can smell something now, and as she wanders from accessory counter to accessory counter to accessory counter, she realizes that what she's smelling is coming from something in her.

Falconetti lived in the modern era and it was easy to believe that what was there in the world was all there was, period. And the only problem was, she was not just Renée Falconetti; she was also Joan of Arc. In the movie she'd already signed the paper conceding that a person couldn't talk with god, or know god, or see anything beyond the palpable facts that were there. That was the necessary capitulation. The next scene was the one in which Joan sees god, and Falconetti also wanted to see god, and wanted to believe, as Joan of Arc believed, that god was there, with her in the world.

She sat on a high wooden chair in the makeshift dungeon, and a man, an actor, was rehearsing the scene in which her hair is cut. As he bent close to her, his arms raised around her face, she could smell the odor from his body and his shirt and she thought to herself that god was in this man, and that through this man she might see god. He was hovering over her as one might imagine the presence of god, hovering, and when she looked up into his eyes she tried to see something or feel something or communicate something, but all she saw were his nose hairs, and she knew this wasn't a disqualification, but it was, in a way, a wall, and she couldn't get past it.

The lights for the shot were set. A man had measured the distance between her face and the camera. She looked around—her feet were in her shoes and the tiles were on the floor and she saw the instruments of torture. The metal plate was still there, leaning against the same wall, and she remembered the plate and she thought about pain, that although pain wasn't god, it was a way to get close to god, and she tried to feel, with as much intensity as possible, the pain that would let her do that. But she didn't want pain; she hated pain, and so she opened her eyes. The director was telling people where to go and what to do, and because of the lights shining down on her, even with her eyes open, she couldn't see. She could hear people moving around beyond the circle of light and then the moving stopped. There was silence. She looked out beyond the light into the darkness, and although the attention of the whole room was directed at her, it was coming from out there, and that's where she looked. Out there. In the film we see the face of Falconetti as her mind twists and stretches in an effort to see, and what she's trying to do is see beyond the facts that had been placed in front of her.

Joan of Arc was taken to the stake, tied in place, and then they lit the pyre. She looked out at that point, and yes, the fire was hot, and I don't want to make it seem as if being burned alive is a trivial thing. Pain isn't trivial. But although she felt the pain, it wasn't the same as suffering. Pain was pain and she saw what it was and she looked beyond that. And the men who were doing the burning thought that turning her into the devil would allow them to keep their authority—and their abuse of authority—hidden. They thought they could rest in peace. And the only problem was this girl who opened her eyes. They did what they could to prevent it, but as Joan stood there, tied to the stake, standing on nothing but fire, she saw that she did have a choice, and before she died she decided.

CAPUCINE

1

Capucine was fifty-seven years old when she killed herself by jumping from a ninth-floor window. First she was born, then she grew up, and after modeling in Paris she began acting in Hollywood movies, one of which was called *Walk on the Wild Side*. In this particular movie she plays a sophisticated prostitute who lives in a brothel run by Barbara Stanwyck, who's in love with her and supports her and lets her have everything she wants except for one small thing: desire.

And then she meets Laurence Harvey. He plays a drifter who falls in love, not with the outer sophistication she wears like a dress, but with a thing inside of her. He's innocent enough to appreciate that thing and want it to be free. As does she. And although she enjoys the expensive wine and the velvet cushions and the pretense of being an artist, she decides to leave the Doll House—that's the name of the brothel—and this becomes the conflict of the story. Barbara Stanwyck won't let her go. Barbara Stanwyck is willing to pay the bills as long as Capucine is willing to be passive and docile, but now desires have been kindled in her, and unfortunately those desires contradict the more powerful desires of Barbara Stanwyck.

The movie is shot in black-and-white and one black night she sneaks down from her upstairs room to rendezvous with Laurence Harvey. Barbara Stanwyck, along with her legless husband, follows her to a Mexican restaurant with a bedroom in the back. In a scene that never made it into the film, everyone is standing around this café. Everyone except for Laurence Harvey, who's in the bedroom waiting for Capucine to join him. That's where she wants to go and she tries to get there by pushing Barbara Stanwyck aside, but in doing so her hand gets taken and held, as if in tar, and she can't seem to pull it away. Her soul, which is what she calls her desire, wants to rise up and burst into the room, but her body, connected to her hand, connected to Barbara Stanwyck, can't move. The character she plays can never reach her longed-for happiness and in the end she's killed, accidentally, shot in a struggle for a gun.

2

Something had begun to develop in Capucine's mind that you might call distrust of desire. Desire came into her life and every time it did it ended badly. So she wanted to keep it "out there." *The Seventh Dawn* was a movie she made with

William Holden, and during the making of the movie she was in love, in a way, with William Holden. And that meant desire, and that meant that even at the height of love she could never completely relax. She couldn't really enjoy her passion because she knew it would all end badly. Even in bed, lying together with their postcoital cigarettes, she waits for her tiny scrap of happiness to falter. And sure enough, when William Holden rolls over to crush out his cigarette she sees in his gesture a crushing out of their love, confirming what she knew would finally happen: failure.

She plays a Malaysian rebel in the movie, and one day after shooting—still with her Malaysian makeup on—she wanders off the set into the town. Pulled by the scent of the late afternoon, she follows her nose to a tree with deep-yellow flowers. Pieces of fruit are rotting on the ground near this tree and the sea is not far off. She sits at the base of the tree, not Buddha-like in a lotus pose, but cross-legged, trying, under the tropical clouds, to erase all trace of desire. She sees desire as a kind of disease and wants to exist without it. When a rain comes, a tropical rain, there she is in her shirt and slacks and instead of running for cover she decides to be still. She decides to force her mind to be calm and wait for the sky to empty itself of confusion. She waits but the rain doesn't stop. The stillness doesn't come. The rain is thick and persistent and she sits in a puddle of mud, waiting and waiting, and finally the rain does stop. As the last sprinkles fall from the sky she decides to stand up. She resolves to enter life and she *does* stand up, soaked to the skin, and she steps over a low row of bushes and walks down the street until she arrives at what seems like a haven.

It's an international hotel, the whole front of which is made of glass. Although she's tall and beautiful she's soaking wet, the Asian makeup dripping down her face, and when she says hello to the man at the door, of course he doesn't recognize her. He stops her from going inside, and she can feel what she calls her soul rising up from the place it normally stays hidden, and she can feel her body get mad. She's taller than the man and as she moves toward him, across the clean carpet, she notices an ashtray on a ledge and she imagines taking that ashtray and smashing the glass of the window. But she doesn't. Instead of breaking the window she turns and begins walking away down the unfamiliar street until finally she stops. Her breathing is fast. She can feel her heart beating, and then suddenly someone is with her. Bill Holden is holding her, soothing her, and also, gently and lovingly, he's reprimanding her for what he makes quite clear has been a silly, inappropriate expression of herself. He wants to know if she's hungry but she's not hungry. He would like her to be hungry but now she's mad, only she's not allowed to be mad, just hungry, and she doesn't know if it's the situation she hates or herself. They're sitting together on a step in front of a doorway—it's a warm night—and William Holden, in his act of comforting her, turns into just another person trying to keep hidden the thing in her body.

This signals to her that their love, which had been comforting, is almost over.

3

In 1965 thirty-four thousand Vietnamese died in Vietnam, and "What's New Pussycat?" became a hit song. In 1965 Malcolm X was murdered in New York, and Timothy Leary coined the phrase "Turn on, tune in, drop out." In 1965 four thousand people were arrested in Watts, and the miniskirt was given its name. In 1965 Norman Morrison, a Quaker, immolated himself on the steps of the Pentagon, and this is what he did.

He drove to Washington in his two-toned Cadillac, and for some reason he brought along his daughter, a baby. He was thirty-two years old and he stood at the gas station pump on the outskirts of town, filling a rusty container with gas. The station attendant—a boy—had pimples on his face, was listening to a Beatles song—"Help!"—on a radio, and the man wanted to bring out whatever it was inside of the boy. He wanted to help but he didn't know how. He bought his daughter an ice cream, then drove to a parking lot along the Potomac and parked beside a construction site near a makeshift shack. The wood on the side of the shack was painted green, deep and green and peeling off, and he looked at the hardened surface and could see beneath that to the living part of paint that was moving and fluid. Looking at the green paint he felt he understood what the paint was doing. The patterns of cracks and the strands of bristle caught in the color weren't part of a message; they simply existed, and he acknowledged that existence. When his daughter cried he picked her up.

Later, standing between two low concrete walls near the five-sided building, he could feel the wind on his face and his daughter in his arms, and he could feel the heat from her body. He set her down and walked about fifteen feet away to where he could concentrate. Then he turned his mind to what he hated: The war. Hopelessness. His own heart. He looked at the flakes of rust in his hand and he saw that all these things were the same. He sat, cross-legged on the hard cement, not like the Buddha, although like the Buddha he wanted to send a message to the world. To ease its pain. He wanted to let whatever it was inside of him come out, and then change it, and by changing that he was hoping everything else would change. He lifted the gasoline can and poured the gas onto his shoulders and his legs. His clothes absorbed the liquid and became heavy with the wetness. The last of the can he sprinkled lightly on his head. He'd kept the matchbook in his closed fist and now he took it and pulled out a wooden match. He lit it. The wind was blowing and he tried to protect the flame, but he couldn't seem to get a grip, literally, on the matchbook—his hands were wet with gas—and the match went out. He tried lighting several matches and it wasn't until the fifth match, and even then the flame was tentative. But that was enough. He'd prepared himself to be a human torch and that's what he became. When the match touched his chest all the anger and hopelessness that was inside of him burst into the heavy air.

4

Capucine was the same age as the man who set himself on fire, and while he was doing that she was making the movie *What's New Pussycat?* She plays one of the women in love with the movie's hero, Peter O'Toole. In the movie true love is impossible, and the reason for living comes down to just one thing: pleasure.

One night some actors who'd been working on the movie invite her out to a party. It's a lavish house with lavish food and she knows a few of the people. But she doesn't feel like talking. So she sits. On a comfortable antique sofa. Her champagne glass is held in a graceful way. There's a lot of talking going on and people are dancing and laughing and at a certain point she realizes that she's doing none of these things. At first this bothers her. At first she feels like joining the rest of the people, acting crazy and wild, but when she tries to get up to do that she seems unable to move. And *feeling* unable to move is like *being* unable to move, and she begins to adjust. She begins to reconcile herself to her immobility; she begins to enjoy the stillness of the deep velvet cushions.

Any kind of giving up contains a certain relief. The tension that exists in whatever struggle there is, vanishes, and it vanishes for her. Why live with this pressure? she thinks, and she seeps deeper into the ease and peace of her surrender. Until someone, someone she barely knows, some man in brightly colored clothes, is standing over her, his hair in his face, asking her to dance. She says no, and he says, "Come on, baby. Let's do it." And she shakes her head but the man persists until finally she has to tell him that she doesn't want to do anything. "I'm perfectly fine here," she says. "Thank you," she says. And the man says, "I know you're fine. You're very fine," and he takes her hand and pulls her up off the luxurious sofa. He leads her to the middle of the room where about fifteen bodies are writhing and twirling, arms and skin and long hair flying in various directions, and in the middle of the middle of this movement she remains perfectly still. Her partner is swinging but she is motionless. She watches as if watching the world itself turn around and around without her.

5

It's raining in Lausanne, quite a few years later. Capucine is in her clean apartment, sitting in a green chair—not like the

Buddha, but sitting—staring off toward the light coming from the window. She's watching the light as it travels from the window to her wrist and the hairs on her wrist. She doesn't feel like moving, and at the same time she wants to. She wants to change what is happening and so resolves to enter into the stream of life, to distract herself from the weight that's crept into the inside of her chest, and so she goes shopping. She wants some meat and she goes to the butcher to buy some. The butcher's face, like his meat, is red and his nose has many holes. He tells her the meat is home-made and she doesn't know what he means. She takes the slab he's wrapped in white paper and as she steps outside the bell rings.

Her favorite street is the old street, with the brown houses and little doors. A man in a suit asks for directions but it's not clear to her where he's going. She steps into a phone booth but forgets who she's going to call. She finds a bench by the street and sits there, watching the shopkeepers close for the evening, and then she gets up and goes home. Halfway there she remembers the parcel of meat still sitting on the bench. But she doesn't go back. It doesn't matter, she thinks, although standing on the sidewalk, near where the cars make a circle, she cries. She cries over the missing meat. She feels a pain in her body, although it's not quite pain; it's a heaviness. She reminds herself that her body is not the problem. This weight, she thinks, is in what she calls her soul, which is not her body. Her body just happens to be what she knows.

She walks across the terrazzo lobby, but instead of taking the elevator up to her floor, she climbs the steps, which are made of cement. They're cool and green and she's able to climb them easily. Inside her room she sits in a chair by the window, looking out through the glass of the window. She can't imagine what a suicide note would say. There's nothing to say. She closes her eyes. The heaviness comes when she thinks of doing something, of acting on the world, because having an effect on the world is impossible, or seems impossible. What she would like is a piece of meat. That's what she thinks, and she stands up. She stands, letting the light from the window fall across her arm and the hairs on her arm and she moves in the general direction of the light. She unlocks the window, opens it, and looks down to the trees and the cars and the people, moving. She can hear them all. She can visualize in her mind the mechanics of lifting first one leg over the railing, then the other, and she doesn't feel any heaviness. She pulls a chair to the window. She puts one foot on the seat of the chair, then the other, and then she stands on the chair, bent slightly, listening to the world as it passes across her face.

GLENN GOULD
IN SIX PARTS

Glenn Gould had a thing about microphones. Not a bad thing; he loved them and loved using them, as long as they weren't in front of people. He preferred them when they were inside windowless, soundproof rooms, because inside those solitary rooms he felt himself enclosed in a kind of bubble. Inside that bubble he could relax and let who he was come out. Although he became attached to the bubble, it wasn't that he liked the bubble so much as he liked the feeling he had when he was there.

1. SOMEONE'S OUT THERE

There he is, standing on the stage. It's not a real stage; it's a recording studio. He's recording piano music in an old Presbyterian church that's been turned into a recording studio, and he's standing on what used to be the pulpit, looking out to what used to be the pews, because he thinks someone is out there. He holds up his hand to shade his eyes and you can see the steam rising off his skin. His hands and arms are red and damp from soaking. He's been soaking his arms in the scalding water of the bathroom sink to get ready to play the piano. But he's not playing. He's standing on what is now a stage, looking for someone he believes is there. He believes someone is out there, but because he can't see anyone he can't prove it.

Three pianos are lined up on the lip of the stage but his chopped-off stool is positioned behind only one. Where he sits. To play. But he can't. His job is to play the piano but he can't get his mind off the person he's convinced is out there, listening. Several men are sitting behind the glass wall of the recording booth but he's not thinking about them. He's thinking about the person he knows is out there, and he knows the person is out there because he can feel that person in his skin.

It's all a distraction, he's aware of that. And the distraction is all in his mind. Fine. So he sits behind the big black Steinway and he touches the tips of his fingers to the smooth white keys. He wants to play, and he's almost ready. Except for the feeling. His eyes and ears are telling him that no one is there, but he believes his feeling. He wants to play but he's distracted by his feeling, so he leans over the piano body and calls out, "I know you're out there." But nothing comes back. So he stands, walks down the five wooden steps that lead off the stage, crosses over the wires on the floor, and goes to the back of the old church. High above him is the vaulted ceiling and he walks under that ceiling to the back stairs and starts to climb. It's a yellow stairway and at first he moves quickly, as if trying to catch the person he believes is there. He starts out by trying to catch someone, but when he's about halfway up he stops, and for a long minute he's motionless, and looking at him then you wouldn't know whether he's trying to catch something, or trying to get away.

At a landing at the top of the stairs he comes to a small door, not even human height, a narrow, half-arched service door, and when he tries it, it opens. He steps in, neck bent, into the darkness of a room. Not room. It's an area, an empty area coated with a layer of dust. There's an arched window near the floor letting in just enough light to see. The ceiling is the same vaulted ceiling he was under before, only here it's low. Which is why he's hunched over. And hunched over, he listens for some sign of something in the room. But the room is absolutely quiet. He's listening, but there's no one there. And then he begins to play. Not the piano, but the music. He begins to play the music that he hears in his mind.

2. THE IDEA OF COLD

This scene begins with Glenn Gould answering his front door. A woman is standing there—a college student probably—holding out a cream-colored envelope. He takes it and feels his chest for a pen, to sign, but there isn't one. The woman sees this and passes him her pen, a blue one. Now the thing about Glenn Gould was that he didn't like to have his hands touched. His hands were his tools—his bread and butter—so when he takes the pen she's offering, he takes it with the very tips of his thumb and finger. When he turns to sign the receipt the woman slips in through the door and closes it behind her. She knows who he is—the famous pianist who quit performing—and so when he passes her back the pen she says, "Great hands." She knows who *he* is but he's not completely sure she's really a messenger; she's talking about scuba diving and the thrill of going under the water, exhorting Glenn Gould to go under the water, and describing how the temperature changes under the water. She's telling him that as one goes deeper and deeper below the surface of the water the temperature gets colder and colder. And Glenn Gould can talk about cold. And he does. Cold is a favorite topic of his and he begins telling her about the North, and what it is to exist in the frozen solitude of the Arctic cold, and that the farther north you go the colder it gets until finally the superfluousness of everyday life is frozen off and you're left with nothing but purity.

All of us create a world—Glenn Gould included—an individual world in which we function. As we live, we establish the boundaries of that world; we get comfortable with certain habits, certain rituals and people, and he's comfortable in a world of purity, or at least a world whose boundaries he can control. And although this woman has no desire to take that away, he feels the need to protect himself. He doesn't like to stand too close, or what he thinks is too close, and people have different ideas about what intimacy is, and Glenn Gould has his idea, whatever it is, and he thinks that the two of them are moving in that direction. He can feel her getting near to the edge of his world, and although he enjoys talking about the cold he can feel her pushing slightly against the skin of his world, and instead of allowing that and the feelings that follow, he acts to avoid it, to avoid the human contact and the fear that goes with it. He opens his door and stands to one side. And she understands—or rationalizes—that yes, he's a great man, etcetera, and he needs his privacy, etcetera, and it's only when she actually starts to walk out the door that he feels the freedom to realize that talking to her is pleasurable, and he says to her, almost accusatorily, "You're leaving?"

Later, he's lying on his back, his head propped on some pillows on the floor, and she's also on the floor, resting on her elbow, looking down at him. He's looking up into her eyes, not looking at any one particular eye but focusing instead on both of her eyes, and seeing both of her eyes at the same time. Like looking at stars. You see the stars in the night sky, but the minute you try to focus on one particular star, it's gone, and it's only when you look slightly away and relax your focus that you're able to see that star. Which is what he's doing, gazing at her, and all the while he's doing it he's talking about parentheses, about how a sentence doesn't really come to life until it encounters a parenthesis (something that changes the trajectory of the sentence (creating a meaning that she understands (as does he, the one who's talking (without focusing) on and on) partly because what he's talking about is how he's talking) without altering its fundamental progress) which gives it a tension and complexity that more resembles life, or if not life, music. And she finds this charming. Gradually a closeness is established, and he feels for the first strong time in his life an inclination to reach out beyond the skin of his world and make contact, and he's about to act on this inclination, but this inclination might take him out of his world, which might leave him, in the end, without any world. So he doesn't act. Instead he closes his eyes and begins to play, not to her but to himself. He begins to play the music that he hears in his mind.

3. THE ISLAND

It's said that Glenn Gould had the ability to practice the piano without actually touching the keyboard. He could hear the piano's notes in his mind, and that's where he rehearsed them. Growing up, an only child, he learned to play, literally, in his mother's lap, sitting between her legs at the piano bench. Because his mother was always there, listening, he was always performing, and the only way he could practice the music was to imagine it.

In those days his parents had a cottage on an island in a lake and one day, in the middle of an argument with his father, Glenn Gould runs across his yard to the yard next to his parent's white house, to an old tire hanging by a rope from a large tree. He holds on to this tire because usually this tire, and swinging on this tire, is able to give him some solace. But this time he finds that all it does is swing, back and forth, and that isn't enough. So he walks out to the wooden pier that was used to dock the motorboat, and he stands on that pier, his dog waiting for a stick to be thrown in the water, but Glenn Gould is looking out. The sky is blue, the sun is not yet hot, and some of the birds in the trees are singing. The water is lapping against the bank of the lake, and looking out to the water, soft and serene, and beyond that, to the mist, even softer, he's waiting for something. He waits but he doesn't hear it. The music doesn't come, and so he turns around and walks back to the thing he was running from.

When he turns back his father is there, sitting in his chair on the wooden deck, one slipper dangling off his foot, doing a crossword puzzle. His mother is sitting in her chair, on the front grass, holding a book, her glasses on the end of her nose. The young Glenn Gould had his own chair and he takes it and carries it off to the side. He sits with both arms resting on the tarnished aluminum arms of his chair, his feet planted firmly on the ground, and sitting there he begins to imagine the music he'd been practicing that morning. At first a few notes, and then a few phrases, and as he works through the difficult passage he begins to hear the music roll out of his brain, or into his brain, and he doesn't know he's moving his fingers, lightly held over the edge of the chair's arm. And he doesn't know he's nodding his head. And because his eyes are closed he can't see his mother watching him, moving her head in time with his, as if she can hear what's inside of him. He's not paying attention to the world outside because he's concentrating on the one that's inside. He's hearing the notes inside his head and only the world inside his head exists for him until, like a dream exploding or like a needle breaking the membrane of skin, he hears his mother's voice.

"Wrong note."

4. EVERY THIRD THOUGHT

Glenn Gould favored solitude because he felt that purity was contaminated by the world, by the competition and judgments of the world, and his goal was to preserve that purity. And he did this, or attempted it, by performing routines and rituals that would bring him into sync with the universe. His goal was the preservation of purity, and so he maintained his isolation, although at the same time he also wanted to enter the contaminating world, and to do that he needed help. Thus the pills and the eccentricities and the naming things. Glenn Gould could quote from several of Shakespeare's plays and one of the lines he quoted came from the end of *The Tempest*. The character Prospero, talking about death, says, "Every third thought shall be my grave." And that's what Glenn Gould did. Every third thought was death. It went something like this: Keys. Muffler. Death. Socks. Door. Death. Car. Wind. Death. Snow. Phone. Death. Throat. Gloves. Death. Bird. Umbrella . . .

5. PROSPERO'S SADDLE

He was coming out of a bank—again a vaulted building—out through the double glass doors and it was bright outside and sunny, and he reached up to pull down his sunglasses, but they weren't on his head, so he tried the pocket of his big navy overcoat. He was busy feeling in his pocket so he didn't notice the woman who came up to him and stood in what was his trajectory, almost touching the buttons of his coat.

He only noticed when the woman, who was younger than she looked, did the gesture of putting finger to lips. And while she was doing this, from behind him, there was a man yelling, something about getting "your goddamn ass into the open." The man was yelling to the woman, who pushed Glenn Gould at the exact moment the man threw what seemed like a wet rag, or something heavy wrapped in a rag, that landed in the street. The woman disappeared around the corner and the man, wearing a lumberjack shirt, mumbled something about dogs or doggone, and with a sheepish defiance dodged his way across the street.

This was the type of encounter—with a stranger—that Glenn Gould found intoxicating. No one was hurt, and when he looked down to see if his coat had been damaged he saw on the cement of the sidewalk a piece of something flashing. He bent down and picked it up. An earring. It was a silver earring in the shape of a western saddle and he held it between his thumb and finger.

His car was parked in the bank's parking lot and he was about to continue on his normal trajectory, getting in his car and driving to his house, but instead he started walking. He started following the path of the woman. Around the corner. The neighborhood was a mixture of stores and houses with the houses set back slightly from the street. In one of the doorways he noticed a figure silhouetted. He also noticed a hotel and a mausoleum and a man with a turban. A bicycle was on its side in a front yard. When he got to the end of the block he looked up and down the street but it was all just people. He realized that he would never find the woman, that she had disappeared, and now she was gone.

He turned back and on the way to his car he happened to look toward the door of the house where the figure had been standing in silhouette. He unlatched the small front gate and walked to the door, which was open, and spoke through a screen into the room of the house which was furnished in shades of tan.

"Hello?" he said. "Is anybody there?"

A television was on but no one was watching.

He tried the handle of the aluminum screen door and it moved, and opened, but he didn't go inside. It was someone's house. But the momentum of events was pushing him or pulling him or he was moving events. At any rate he walked in, saying several warning hellos as he walked back to the area where the light was brightest. There was a narrow kitchen and beyond that a small, carpeted room and that's where she was, the woman from the bank. She was standing, her arms folded across her chest.

Glenn Gould held out the earring but at that distance and with that light the woman didn't see what he was doing. It looked as if he was approaching her and was going to pinch her. He held the earring for her to see and when she saw it shine she put her fingers out in the shape of pinching and she took the earring from him. Then she put it into her ear. Then she thanked him.

"No, no," he said, taking a step back, saying that really, what he did was nothing.

And that's when she said to him, "May I shake your hand?"

She didn't know who he was. She didn't know that in Toronto by this time he was something of a celebrity. She just wanted to thank him for his thoughtfulness. She didn't know that his hands were famously cold.

"May I shake your hand?"

"Of course," he said, and he held out his hand for her to take it.

6 . SILENT NIGHT

Glenn Gould was happy to admit it: he was a hypochondriac. There were the pills, the blood pressure tests, the constant worry, and there were also home remedies. When he felt a numbness along the left side of his body he thought he could cure himself, and his cure for the lack of feeling in his body was to go under water. Hot water. He ran hot water into his bathtub and took off his clothes, which left him standing on his small white rug with nothing but the translucent whiteness of his skin. That and the patches of hair. He then eased himself into the tub and, with a candle burning beside him on the toilet seat lid, soaked himself. Because the water was hot he had to lower himself slowly, putting his feet up on one end of the tub, his hands braced against the other. He gradually lowered himself, getting used to the heat of the water, his body going farther and farther into the water until finally he took a deep breath of air and then slid his whole head down. He kept it there under the water until he got dizzy, letting the heat penetrate into his brain, thinking it was his brain that needed blood.

One day he's in his bed, books piled up around him and with him and he can't seem to get to sleep. It's daytime. Normally he sleeps during the day, and it's day now, but he can't seem to get comfortable. It's his left side. It's not his mind. It's his body. And his ears. That's another thing he worries about, his hearing. He's worried now, not scared exactly, but he wants the feeling to go away, now, and when it doesn't he feels that his body is acting against his wishes. He's taken the pills that usually work and now they don't. It's his left side. Not his mind. It actually does exist. Not a big problem, he's pretty sure, and tells himself it's not that bad, but he feels—or doesn't feel, that's just it—he doesn't have feeling on his whole left side. And yes, he believes that his life is lucky, and that his luck has something to do with his connection to music, and the purity of music. He feels connected to the world of music and protected by that world, and he expects to be spared. He tries to avoid this new, unwanted situation by turning again to music, by closing his eyes and invoking his music, by hearing the music in his head. He closes his eyes to hear it, but this time his refuge fails him. This time the music doesn't come.

GOOD WORLD

1. GIRL IN A FIELD

There's the field. It's made of rocks and grass and a few bushes. And a girl, pure potential, is running in this open field. I call her pure potential because she's young and she's full of the euphoria of possibility. This was 1949, after the war, when optimism was in the air—about victory and technology—and the girl is in the middle of a scene that ought to be perfect. She's running through the field with her cousin and sister, running and laughing and pausing occasionally to pick up stones. They're looking for a certain kind of stone, an egg-shaped stone, and the girl wants to find one.

Gus, her cousin, and Barbara, her sister, are older than she is and the world they inhabit is the world that she wants, and she believes that it's possible to enter that world if she can find a perfectly egg-shaped stone. And when you look directly at something, like a star, you can't see it, but if you look slightly away you do, and that's what she does, and when she finds what she thinks is a perfectly egg-shaped stone she tries to show them. Holding the stone in her hand she calls to them, trying to get their attention, but they keep running and yelling as if they don't even hear.

I said this girl is pure potential, and that's fine, but the potential isn't getting her anywhere. She feels the powerlessness of youth, and the inability of youth to affect the world, and although she seems to be a carefree girl running through a field we see that something else is happening. We can hear the trembling in her voice when she says, holding up her stone, "Look at this one." When she says, "Look at mine," we can tell she's waiting for some change to happen.

But Gus and Barbara keep running, and all the girl can think to do is wait, to stand there in the afternoon sun hoping that someone at some point will come to her. And when her cousin does finally run over and stop in front of her, panting, she shows him her egg-shaped rock. He takes it, looks at it, and she watches him looking, hoping he'll see the goodness of the rock, and she's confused when he says, "Not bad," and tosses it aside. "Here," he says, and he reaches down, picks up another rock, a more egg-shaped rock, and he says something about aerodynamics and the science of flight, and then he throws this rock as far as he can. And then he runs off.

And that's when we see the girl, alone in the field, her head down, scanning her peripheral vision for an oblong stone hidden in the galaxy of stones and pebbles. That's when we see that the field is almost entirely flat except for a grassy knoll, a little greener than the rest of the field, and as the girl moves closer to the grassy area we start to get worried. We can imagine what might happen. We can probably anticipate the abandoned well hidden in the green grass. When suddenly the girl disappears we're pretty sure she's fallen into the hole.

2. LAIKA THE DOG

Once upon a time there was a dog that wanted to be an astronaut. A cosmonaut really, because she was a communist dog, a Siberian husky taken in and trained by Soviet scientists. Her original name was Little Curly but they called her Laika, which means "Barker," because she made a lot of noise. And she made a lot of noise because she wanted to be the first dog in space.

This was 1957. *Sputnik* was about to be launched, and because there wouldn't be much moving around in the capsule, the scientists were looking for a dog who could learn to be still, and Laika was willing to be that dog. She was willing to learn, or try to learn, her lessons, and by lessons I mean the repeated behaviors that were meant to become habit.

Aristotle called habit the foundation of virtue, and what he meant I think is that the value of an action lies partly in its ability to repeat itself, to become something more than random. You don't hear the word "virtue" much anymore, and the word "habit" usually refers to something unwanted or out of control. But Aristotle, from the vantage point of ancient history, saw the development of habit as a way to move toward happiness.

And that was fine with Laika except the habits she seemed to develop were not the right habits. She excelled at running and barking and playing around, but the *Sputnik* people were looking for a dog to be still, and although Laika wanted to oblige, her natural inclination, if there is such a thing, was to constantly be moving. She tried to contain or control that impulse, but there were other dogs who seemed to control it better.

So on the day they were to select which dog would explore the universe, Laika was nervous. She was nervous when the young scientist took her to the open field behind the barracks and told her to sit. She could see the men by the fence watching her with their stopwatches and their notepads, and when her leash was removed and the scientist started walking away she thought, Okay . . . and she tried to remain perfectly still, but as the young scientist continued walking, Laika felt the desire to move, and she tried to contain it or fight it or work through it—she tried to stop and concentrate—and sometimes she did, and when the desire began to fade she thought she was over it, that she'd turned over a new leaf, but there was no new leaf, the desire was still there, bigger than ever, and she began to think she shouldn't fight it, that maybe she *should* move, that her muscles might atrophy, or that the man might abandon her; a million logical thoughts made it necessary for her to get up and move.

Which would be a huge relief.

Or so she thought. Of course when she did finally move it wasn't that wonderful or that fulfilling, but by then it was too late, her dream would not come true; some other dog would go into space and she would remain exactly what she would always be, a loud and useless dog.

Except that the scientists were looking for more than just stillness. They could see her desire, and they valued that desire, and so she was the one who was chosen to be launched into space. And although there are several versions of what actually happened to her up there, they all boil down to basically the same thing. The batteries of her life support system would last only so long, and the scientists, not wanting to inflict a painful death, inserted into the last of her food supply some poison. When she was down to her final meal the poison entered her body, and although the famous satellite remained in orbit for 162 days, after about a week Laika was already dead.

3. ANNE AND RICHARD

We see two people, Richard and Anne, a man and a woman—characters in a play. The man is dressed in black, and although the woman is wearing a white wedding-type gown she seems to be on the verge of crying. Until she notices the man. He's bent over, hair stringy, bowing almost as he offers her some thing he's holding in his hand. She immediately turns her back, clenches her fist, tells him to get out of her sight, and from her tone of voice we can tell that she hates this man.

He says something about understanding her loss, then immediately tells her he loves her more than any husband could love, and as if it's happened a thousand times she feels a familiar sickness rising up from her belly. At this point she would like to walk away and escape from whatever the man is planning, but instead she stands there, and the man pries open the fingers of her fist and places in her hand a ring.

It's an exquisite example of late sixteenth-century craftsmanship and she would probably want the ring except for one thing: her contempt. She throws the jewel into the dirt. And the funny thing is, he walks over and matter-of-factly retrieves it, as if he knew what would happen. Like part of a choreography he goes back to her, admits that he killed her husband, and tells her the reason he killed her husband was his love for her. And that's when she spits into his face.

The woman knows that spitting at him is just the beginning of a whole succession of tortures she would like to inflict, including tearing out his heart and stuffing it into his mouth. But the man just wipes his face. Patiently. And that's what I mean by choreographed—he's slow and methodical, and his patience bestows a kind of power to his actions, which flow from one to the other until he's presenting her with a knife. He has a knife in his coat and he holds it out to her, saying that she, if she wants to, can kill him.

But it's against her principles to kill another human be-ing, however inhuman he might be, and when she ignores the knife, he takes it himself, raises it, and holding it to his own breast, offers to kill himself if that would make her happy. He's full of bravado, but he's also quite convincing, partly because he's so focused on her, observing her smallest movement, including the movement of the muscle buried beneath her smooth, round cheek.

He takes her silence as an invitation, and he steps for-ward, slowly, gradually, bringing his face closer to hers, moving in such an incremental way that she's not completely sure that he actually is moving, until, with his face almost touching hers, she closes her eyes, aware that his lips are pressing against her lips, and for about a second, a long sec-ond, her eyes stay closed.

And then they pop open as if she suddenly wakes up.

And what she suddenly wakes up to is the question in her mind: Why am I kissing this man? or Why am I allow-ing myself to be kissed? or Where is my anger? She's con-fused. She's been trained to be a "good person," and yes, he is an older man, and a powerful man, and although she has to think about her future, she hates what is happening. She hates him. She wasn't acting when she spat at him, and yet now when she needs to fight, the desire to fight has aban-doned her.

So she wants to start again. She thinks she knows what the problem is, what she needs to do, and yes, maybe it didn't work this time, it wasn't right this time, but she's full of optimism that given another chance she will do it differently. One more time and she knows she can stop the repetition.

Like Aristotle. For Aristotle, an action repeated again and again becomes habit, and by virtue of the repetition it becomes a direction, a movement, and implicit in that movement is a force, a pulling or pushing against the conflicting impulses of other habits. And so we have to be careful. Each time around, the rut is carved a little deeper.

Which is why they're still here. Anne and Richard. Same people, slightly different location. He still walks up to her, and even before he opens his mouth she hates his smell. Even though he's probably wearing some sort of perfume, she hates it so much that when he offers her the ring she throws it into the gutter. When he limps over, exaggerating his deformity, she feels no pity. She sees exactly what he is, and when he has the temerity to offer his love, that's when she collects the liquid in her mouth and spits.

And yes, she's worried that it's happening in the same way because she would like it to happen in a different way. She understands that now is the time to alter events, to focus her hatred and direct it at him, and what she needs is something after which all that she does will be different. She looks at her hands. They're not trembling but she wishes they would be trembling because then they'd be filled with resolve. She's waiting for her hands to rise up, and when he presents her with the knife, she thinks, Okay. Now she has the opportunity to change the course of events, to throw her world into a new orbit, and what she has to do is take the knife he's offering and plunge it into his heart.

But killing another human being is not something she does. She doesn't do that. And so, as if on cue, he places the point of the knife to his own neck, and what's she going to do?

"I want to start again."

That's what she says.

"Okay," he says.

4. THE MO-TEL IDEA

In 1929 they invented the motel. They didn't actually invent it; it just happened. Some man put a sign up on the side of the road and the idea was born. It was able to be born because of the existence of the car, and the highway. People were suddenly driving cars and a need to sleep existed where it hadn't been before, a vacuum that was filled by this thing called a motor hotel. The idea of a place to stay along the road wouldn't have been thought of before. You couldn't have planned it. But once the highways were there, something that hadn't even been a possibility, became necessity. Or more precisely, habit. A circumstance creates a need which is satisfied by a certain action, which is repeated and repeated until pretty soon it's part of life. A man in San Luis Obispo is credited with coining the word "mo-tel." And maybe he did, or maybe he just had the biggest sign. Maybe the idea was floating in the air, and when it landed, there it was. The whole process is fairly unpredictable. People need a place to sleep. They want to drive across the country and not get wet when they get out of their cars. I wouldn't want to call it a momentous event in the history of the world, but it's an example of a change that can only happen when the requisite pieces are in place.

5 . ANNE AND RICHARD

Let's go back to the two people, the man and the woman. The woman, Anne, realizes that if she's going to change the course of events she needs to put the pieces in place, she needs to act now and create a beginning and the only problem is: she doesn't know what to do. He offers her the ring and she thinks, Yes. Okay. The ring. Should she take it? She doesn't think she should take his ring and yet the only alternative she can think of is throwing it down onto the cobblestones. Same as always.

And when he offers her the sword she thinks, Yes . . . Okay. The sword. She takes the sword. He bends down in front of her, pulls the material away from his neck, revealing the pale skin of a man who has never been loved, and she resolves that, yes, her life means more than his, and she tries to believe that. This is her opportunity and she tries to see herself thrusting the sharp blade through the skin and into the muscles and the organs, and she's looking down on him, with his eyes lowered, and she sees that he's just another person, some man who probably wants what all men probably want, and what is she supposed to do? Killing him isn't going to change her life. She knows it's her attitude that will change her life; her mind and her heart are the things that will change her life, and they're not changing. She waits awhile, giving them a chance to change, and when finally nothing happens, she gives up.

She's silent. It's already gone too far. She would like to be asleep in one of those cozy motels on the side of the highway, but there aren't any motels for her. She was hoping she would have more time, but there is no time. The present has become the future and she can see it. She can see what's going to happen because it's happening now. He's standing, close enough for her to notice his breathing, and his smell, and his smooth face, moving closer and closer to her face until finally she doesn't want to be kissing him but that's what has to be happening. It's not that she wants to give up, but fighting has proven to be futile, and so she resigns herself to the idea of a next time, that next time things might change, that next time she might be free of this man, and the only problem is: now is the next time. And so the kiss goes on and on and she has no choice but to let herself be kissed. This is where she is, she thinks, and there's nothing she can do.

The girl who'd fallen into the well is now about ninety feet down. The earth opened up and she fell, hitting the sides of the shaft, falling until she came to the place where the well changes direction. And that's where she's stuck, cut and bruised and it seems like a long time before she hears her parents, standing at the top of the well, calling her name. She can't see them but she can tell they're hoping she's alive and that nothing has changed. She's also hoping that nothing has changed, and that her parents will take her away from the darkness and the cold.

The opening of the well is only fourteen inches across, and the shaft is too unstable for anyone to come down after her, so what her parents do is lower a rope. And she can feel this rope brush against her shoulder, and although she wants help, a rope is not the kind of help she has in mind, and when she hears her parents ask if she can tie the rope around her waist she starts crying. Partly she wants to reach out to take the rope, and partly she wants her parents to climb down, wrap her in their arms, and carry her out of the hole and up into the world of happiness.

We probably think that won't happen. We can probably predict that she'll die in the well, which she does. Painlessly, they say. And although the well is almost completely black, I can picture her, down there, holding on to an egg-shaped rock, her bent legs stuck in the mud, half expecting something to happen, at first, and then not expecting anything. This is where she is, she thinks, and she can tell that she's hurt and that if anything is going to change it'll have to start changing now. And so she gives up waiting. At that point the paralyzed little girl turns into a different girl, a girl who lets the rock fall from her hand, who reaches out, takes the rope dangling in front of her, and with it ties a bow around her stomach, a single knot like the kind she ties her shoes with. She ties herself in the rope like a package.

And then she calls out. "Hello?"

"Hello?" she says.

And this is what I mean by habit. Aristotle indicated that happiness is a habit; it isn't random. A single act that fosters happiness is fine as far as it goes but it's only a beginning, a necessary beginning, and although the girl in the well tied only one small knot, for her that was a beginning.

7. LAIKA'S DREAM

Laika, the dog, had been chosen to be the first dog in space, and so she was feeling the exhilaration of possibility. She knew about pure potential because she was feeling it, and the only problem was: nothing was happening. I wouldn't want to say she wasn't happy in her world, but she wasn't completely happy. She was waiting for some lesson or direction or purpose.

And then one day she was led, out of her basement room, into an elevator, and up into the *Sputnik* module. She was strapped into her padded compartment, connected by wires to the black box recorder, and then the photographers came. Lights were shined in her face, and because she understood what was wanted of her, she made the face we think of as a smile. Photos show her, one ear up, one flopped over, her paws crossed, happily surveying what we suppose is the possibility of life in space.

And then the lights were taken away. The scientists said good-bye, the capsule hatch was closed, and Laika found herself sealed inside the darkness. And it was dark. And quiet. And it wasn't long before she felt the vibrating of the booster rocket, the explosion, and then she felt herself being pulled, by the force of gravity on the one hand, and by the force of the missile rising up. The next thing she knew she was floating in space, out of the bonds of the atmosphere.

After about six days of orbiting Earth she'd eaten her way to the end of her food supply, and being a dog, one thing Laika knew was food, so I think she probably knew her food was tainted, that she'd been poisoned, and that she would die. And at first she couldn't believe it. There must be some mistake, she thought. Don't forget, it was almost entirely black up there, so she was blind, and there were no smells in her air supply, and she couldn't move, and the only thing she could hear was her own breathing, amplified by her special helmet. She thought she was contributing to the collective knowledge of the human race, but she wasn't sure. She felt light-headed, either from the weightlessness or the poison, and in her soporific state she had a dream.

In her dream she's riding in a railroad car, and when the train slows down she jumps off and starts running down the tracks, trying to get away from something in the train. She comes to a small, quiet town—it's night—and when she hears voices chasing her she runs to the nearest door, squeezes through a crack in the door, and finds herself in the kitchen of a small house. A man and woman are sitting at a table near a stove and when they look at her it's as if they expected her to be there. She hears a knocking on the door; a soldier comes into the kitchen. He's young, and he lifts his hand to strike the woman, and Laika, pressing her nose against the wooden floor, is keeping perfectly still, perfectly quiet, knowing somehow that unless she is perfectly still, the man and the woman will die. A small beetle crawls across the floor, and she leaves it alone. The soldier changes his mind. He spits, and then walks away.

I wouldn't call it a happy dream exactly, but it's basically optimistic. Laika believed Aristotle's dictum about habit and happiness, and because she lived in the previous century, the century of optimism, she thought her actions would be a beginning. When she realized she was going to die she didn't mind that much because she was dying with the hope that a single act would make the world better. A hope that we, in this century, have our doubts about. We live in the future she believed would come, but we've never really kicked the habits of violence and greed. While Laika dreamed of changing the world, our dream, at this point, would be just to have a dream.

And that's why I'm thinking about Laika. Because I can almost imagine her feeling of powerlessness and optimism. Sitting in a dark spaceship, a microphone tied to her neck, the poison working its way into her system, not knowing what to do, and with nothing to rely on but habit, it's out of habit that she stops, and she concentrates, and her breathing slows, and she becomes aware, gradually, of her heartbeat. At first there's just the feeling of the microphone on her skin, and her heart, beating, and because she's harnessed in place there's nothing to do but let her heart keep beating, let the blood keep pumping, let the signals from her heart flow as directly as possible into the small black box. Because she believes that someone will be listening, she stays alive as long as she can, hoping the message emanating from the heart is clear, wanting the world to hear, not just the ticking of a heart, but the possibility it might contain.

CRIMES AT MIDNIGHT

A CAR EXPLODES

At the beginning of the movie *Touch of Evil*, a car explodes. Actually, it takes about three minutes, but we know the car is going to explode because we see a pair of hands reach out from the shadows and place a bomb in the trunk of the car. We see two people walk to the car, open the doors, and get in. Rudy Linnaker is a businessman and Zita is a local dancer. They emerge from the go-go nightclub, get into the shiny 1958 Chrysler convertible, and as they drive across the Mexican border, Rudy isn't talking and Zita is beginning to worry that maybe she's done something wrong. She's always doing something wrong, it seems, and she wants to know what it is.

"Rudy?" she says. "What's the matter? You're not mad at me are you?" But Rudy isn't talking. He's driving, slowly, and Zita is telling him, "Rudy. You have to talk to me, Rudy." But Rudy is quiet. And because the car is a luxury car, it's also quiet, and Zita, in the silence, can hear some kind of noise. "In my head," she says. "There's a noise." And by the time they pull up to the border checkpoint she's positive she's hearing something. "There's a noise," she says. "I hear a noise. I swear I hear a ticking."

Not far away, hovering in the middle distance, a woman named Susan and her fiancé or boyfriend, a man named Vargas, are leaning up against an old adobe building. I should say *he* is leaning, because it's his back that's against the wall. Susan is played by Janet Leigh and she's pressing up against him in her Hollywood sweater, letting her desires show. She's in the middle of what she thinks is a romantic getaway and Vargas is having a little trouble with that. He has a pencil-thin mustache and he's having a little trouble with her mouth in the shape of a possible kiss. He's saying, "Slow down, Susie. People are watching."

But she's filled with the idea of romance and desire and so she moves closer.

"Whoa, Susie. Please," he says. "We just stepped over the border."

And playing the part of this woman, Janet Leigh can feel the beginning of what she calls unhappiness, and in an effort to elude that unhappiness, she reaches into her purse. She pulls out a small silver camera, but before she can get the lens cap off he's taken it out of her hand, and he's telling her that it's too dark, that it won't work. Putting the camera into her purse, he says to her, "What about that sundae? I promised you a sundae. Don't you want that chocolate sundae?"

Back in the big Chrysler, stopped at the border, Rudy Linnaker says he has nothing to declare. Zita, on the other hand, is getting more adamant about the noise. "Don't you hear it?" she says. "I definitely hear it." But the guards, be-cause she's an exotic dancer, don't listen. Plus she's been drinking. Plus the man driving the big convertible owns half the American side of the town. So even though she declares that she hears a ticking, that she can't get rid of the ticking, they let the car drive off.

Zita is young and she's drunk and she's a stripper, but she's not stupid; she hears a noise and demands that Rudy stop the car. Rudy doesn't know she's not stupid because he thinks everybody's stupid, so he keeps driving until he's forced to slow down by some people crossing in front of him. At which point Zita slides over, opens the door, and tries to get out. And she almost does. Her purse does; her white purse falls onto the asphalt but Rudy doesn't let her get away. He grabs her, pulls her in, holds her in place. Even though he won't talk to her, he holds her. Even when she's screaming, "Let me go, I'm getting out of this car," he tells her she's not going anywhere. He holds her down, twisting her wrist, telling her to sit still and keep her mouth shut. "Keep your big mouth shut," he says.

And yes, she does have a large mouth, but she refuses to keep it shut. "I won't keep it shut. I hear a ticking," she says. "There's a ticking, I swear. I hear this ticking in my head. There's this noise in my head and I can't stand it."

"Well," he says, "you have to stand it."

And that's when the car explodes.

The Third Man is a movie set in Vienna just after the war. In it, Joseph Cotten has come to the divided city to start a new life, and also to find his friend, a man named Harry Lime, played by Orson Welles. I never knew Vienna just after the war, but from the movie, or what I remember of the movie, the city was mostly destroyed, and in this scene Joseph Cotten has gone to a fairly ragged-looking nightclub to meet a police inspector, a man named Callahan or Calloway, and he's standing at the entrance of the nightclub, looking into the smoke and darkness—pianola music in the background—and he feels a hand on his shoulder. The inspector introduces himself and they walk together to a table. Calloway offers to buy the drinks and Cotten, who plays a man named Holly Martins, doesn't mind a free drink. He's a writer of westerns or pulp westerns, a failed writer in his own eyes who wants to change his life. And so they sit, talking about Santa Fe and the Wild West and it's all perfectly friendly, and the bourbon starts to flow, and because Cotten, at that moment, is a little short of money, he enjoys the drinking and they keep drinking, although I should make it clear that Cotten is the one who keeps drinking. Calloway prefers sobriety and control. He's looking for information about Harry Lime, who he believes is a criminal, and because he thinks that Cotten can help he asks a lot of questions, urging

Cotten to drink, trying to find out what Cotten knows about Harry Lime, but Cotten knows nothing. And instead of leaving it at that, instead of calling it a day, Calloway goes one step further; he tries to convince Joseph Cotten that Harry Lime is a murderer.

Because Joseph Cotten loves Harry Lime, or the memory of Harry Lime, he doesn't like listening to what he believes are lies, slanderous lies about his old friend and hero, his longtime hero. And as Calloway proclaims the litany of Lime's supposed crimes it gets to the point where Joseph Cotten hates it. First not liking, then hating. And there they are, sitting at the table, and by the third or fourth drink, when the stiff-lipped policeman intimates that Harry Lime is partly responsible for the deaths of a number of innocent people, Cotten starts to get aroused. Not sexually, but the feeling in his body is not unlike a kind of sexual excitement, and it's hard to contain, and as Calloway keeps up his assault, Cotten's excitement begins feeding on itself, and growing, and because he's a man who's looking for a different kind of life he tries to maintain some equanimity, tries to accept the possibility of another point of view, tries to control himself. But he can't stand hearing what he doesn't want to hear, and instead of standing it, instead of feeling the unpleasant pain or fear that's happening, he distracts himself by getting mad. As long as some thing or some one is out there to rage at, the thing he can't stand conveniently disappears from his consciousness, momentarily. If you would ask him what it is he can't stand he wouldn't mention the sensations in his body or his aversion to those sensations. He'd look at Calloway and see that Calloway is the thing he can't stand.

And we don't actually see the fist flying through the air. What we notice are the chairs breaking into pieces and Calloway, lying on the floor, holding the side of his face. Joseph Cotten walks out the door. End of scene. But earlier in that scene when the two men met I believe there was a close-up. It only lasted a few frames but in it you could see the police inspector's hand take hold of Cotten's arm or coat, and pull. It's an insignificant action in itself, but that innocuous little tug is the beginning. From there a world of resistance is set into motion which neither man notices because neither man is paying attention. Calloway is thinking about what he wants, and Joseph Cotten is thinking about preventing what Calloway wants, and so they notice neither the tug nor the reaction to the tug. Cotten, if you would ask him, would say that, because he's in a strange town, at an unknown juncture in his life, he doesn't mind a little direction, and yet in that close-up shot of the hand on the coat you can see the tension in the coat, the indication of hidden defiance. Something in him refuses to be pulled. And yet at the same time he wants to be pulled, wants to know the truth about Harry Lime, and so, although the material of his coat remains intact, he in a way is torn.

THE PULL OF FALSTAFF

Orson Welles, at a point in his career when he was no longer the *enfant terrible*, at least outwardly, directed a movie based on the fictional life of John Falstaff, and in the movie he plays Falstaff. Wearing a false nose and a padded belly, he makes himself king of this particular nightclub, charming his way through life, drinking and dissembling and ruling, not with force, but with misdirection and bravado. Although the job of getting what he wants seems to just happen, magically, in actuality he's making it happen, and partially he's making it happen by what he's willing to do. If being a dissolute drunk is the way to fight resistance, then that's what he does. And from that position he maintains his influence over friends, enemies, and also the young Prince Hal.

I should say he *tries* to maintain his influence over the young prince. He needs the collaboration of this man who is destined to be king, and although in the movie there is no pulling of a coat, Prince Hal, the future monarch, can feel the tugging. Falstaff, his old friend, is pulling him, not maliciously, but pulling him, away from a life of authority, into a life of frivolity and dissipation, and there's a resistance in Hal. He's a man of resistance. We don't see it at first, and indeed he carouses and cavorts with the best of the merrymakers, but even as he's reveling in his own decadence, he's holding something back.

And not just with Falstaff. He's also resisting the responsibility of power. His birth and his talent are pushing him into the world of action, but he refuses to engage with that world, assuming he'll be free from the pressure of that world, but really it's the pressure of his own desire. He dreams of the life he wants, but makes no move to get it, and Orson Welles, insinuating himself in the gap of this ambivalence, is able to exert control.

But it's only a provisional control, so Orson Welles is worried. He can see his protégé not wholly committed to the life he's promulgating, and in an effort to draw Hal deeper into his orbit, he becomes wittier and jollier and also more demanding. There's the desire to maintain the allegiance of the prince, and there's his dread of possible betrayal. And that possibility, rather than urging caution and delicacy, festers in him, and causes him to press the limits of his young friend's loyalty. He creates a desperation in himself, and in that desperation makes several mistakes—really one mistake with several parts. He assumes that he is the center of the story, and also, that the only way to change what's happening is to corrupt what's happening, and so he corrupts himself.

The way Welles plays the part, Falstaff is a kind of magician, and it's hard to see what he's doing because he's doing so much. Like any good magician he wants to seduce his audience, to distract them momentarily, to make them blink and so allow the experience of amazement to proceed as if by fate. Welles, like a master of fate, remains aloof and inscrutable, but if you could take away the presence of the prince, and take away the other actors and the costumes and the scenery and language, so that Orson Welles, the man, is standing alone on an empty stage, and you could see his face and the contours of his face, the thing you would see is fear.

OPEN WINDOW

Janet Leigh is in her hotel room, one flight up, walking back and forth in front of the large, open window. On the street below her, vendors are peddling shoeshines and firecrackers, and young boys carry cigar boxes filled with chewing gum. People are crossing the border on foot, stopping at whiskey bars and change-making offices, casting shadows across the doorways of cut-rate divorce lawyers. Janet Leigh is taking the clothes from her suitcase, putting them on the newly made bed, then taking them back to the suitcase. She's doing this because she's confused, and she's confused because Vargas has left her alone.

In the middle of walking back and forth in the small room, she stops, looks up, and although she can't see, she knows that someone is watching. She prides herself on knowing when someone is watching her and she knows a man—definitely a man—is standing or sitting or huddled in the darkened room across the street staring at her. She's wearing a white sleeveless blouse and a white slip, and she doesn't know who it is but she knows she doesn't like it. But because the window has no curtain or shade there's no escape unless she hides in the bathroom, and she doesn't want to hide. She wants to talk.

She stands at the open window and, pretending she doesn't mind being looked at, yells across the narrow street. "Here I am. Okay? Take a good look, okay? Are you happy now?" But she's not happy. She tries to forget whoever it is and go about her business, but even the business of walking back and forth has become *his* business. Whatever she does she's doing it for him and she hates that. She tries to just get dressed, to concentrate on putting on her clothes and forgetting about anything else, but the man is not only across the street, he's also in her mind, and she can't get him out. She is unable to get dressed without getting dressed for him. And since she can't forget about him, she tries to engage him, directly. "Are you there?" she yells. "Hello? The show's over, okay? You've had your look. That's all there is. There's nothing more." And then she waits for some response.

But there is no response. And she would like at least to look back equally. If he were illuminated then she would see him and there wouldn't be a problem. She wouldn't care. But she can't see him and she does care and . . . "Who are you, anyway?" she says. "It won't hurt to talk to me. You can't just hide there and not talk to me."

Again, no response, and she finds the lack of it excruciating, partly because she wants to be acknowledged, and partly because she's wondering what the man is thinking. She worries about her posture, and the backs of her arms, and she feels she is in a spotlight. Although there is no spotlight she feels she is in one, illuminated for all the world, for everyone but herself, and although she would like to forget about everyone else and tend to herself, she feels these eyes focusing on her. She can't concentrate on what she's doing because she's concentrating on what the eyes out there are looking at. Not even her, but her body, this thing. "You want to look?" she calls out. "Fine." And she unbuttons her blouse and opens it to reveal her bra. "It's yours," she says. "You can have it." But whoever it is stays hidden, and Susan, suddenly chilly, looks around and sees, in front of her face, a string hanging from the lightbulb lighting the room. She pulls a chair over, stands on it, and using some underwear to protect her hand, unscrews the bulb. She steps off the chair, up to the window, and, as hard as she can, she throws the piece of glass through the air toward the room across the street. Her throw falls short and the bulb shatters against the side of the building.

That's when Vargas enters the room.

"What are you doing in the dark, Susie?" he says. But before she can speak he reminds her that, although the bomb may have been planted in Mexico, it was . . .

"Fine," she says. And this is what I mean by not standing it. And what she does to avoid standing it is walk toward the door leading down the stairs into the lobby of the moderately priced border town hotel. She's wearing her slip and her unbuttoned white blouse. No shoes. No skirt. And you might think that she doesn't know what she's doing, but she's doing what she can. She wants to change what's happening. Because he's an important official investigating an important crime he can't have his girlfriend or fiancée parading around in her underwear, so he steps forward, and for a brief but focused moment looks into her face.

IN A LOOP

Joseph Cotten walks up a curving flight of stairs, knocks on a door at the top of the stairs, and there's no response. Harry Lime had sent him the address and he's gone to that address and when he knocks again, and there's no response, he calls in through the closed door. That's when a man appears in the hallway holding a broom, speaking a kind of half-German, half-English. This man, the concierge, agrees to show him the apartment, and in fact he gives Cotten a royal tour of the several rooms, talking about Harry Lime, but in a way that doesn't coincide with Cotten's conception of Harry Lime. And although Cotten is listening, partly, he's having a little trouble. There's a compartment in his mind and he wants to fill that compartment with information, but he doesn't want any information spilling over into other, already established compartments. And as the man goes into greater and greater detail about Harry Lime's specific activities, Cotten finds himself less and less able to understand the actual words the man is uttering.

That's when Anna walks in through the open door. She's tall and beautiful and when the concierge sees her standing on the dark rug in her black dress he immediately begins sweeping the already quite clean parquet floor, making his way out of the room. "I knew Harry," she says, and she makes a mysterious gesture which Cotten doesn't quite understand, but he doesn't ask her to elaborate because in a way she's saving him from the man, or from what the man was saying. Plus, he finds her attractive, plus she's a friend of Harry's, plus she can speak English, which she does as she takes the arm of his coat, and pulling him, leads him down the curving marble staircase.

He follows her through the rubble of the city to a nightclub and through the nightclub to a backstage dressing room filled with hats and dresses and bottles of perfume. Out in the nightclub he can hear men talking to dancers, drinking and laughing, and although Anna is also laughing, Joseph Cotten can see it's a laughter behind which something is hiding. He watches her as she applies her makeup and adjusts her wig, and he wants to reach out, to put his hand on the skin of her shoulder, and so he walks to her. But he doesn't reach out. And when she stands and faces him he doesn't smile, doesn't make a joke, he doesn't ask her about Harry Lime; instead he begins moving, slowly, around her in a circle. And gradually she starts moving, equally slowly, around him, so that they begin walking around each other, literally in circles, walking as if they're in an art museum, each person in a separate orbit, each noticing some separate aspect of the other. He's looking at her earrings and where her hair meets her temple, and she's looking at his nose and the space between his collar and his neck. And whatever sensations they're feeling as they circle each other, they're reacting to those sensations in basically the same way.

What they're doing is stalling.

Earlier, when they'd walked through the crowded nightclub with the half-dressed dancers on the raised stage, Cotten turned his face away from the stage. He turned away, not because he wasn't interested in seeing half-dressed women, but because he was. He wanted to look, but he didn't want to experience the discomfort of being looked *at*. He'd spent some time in striptease places and although this wasn't a striptease place, he'd developed a certain procedure which entails going in, sitting down, and when he looks at the dancer—always one particular dancer—he feels that he's the one being scrutinized. There's a partially naked person in front of him and he's busy thinking, Where does she want me to look? or, Does she want me to look? Does she want me to look at her face because I appreciate who she is as a person, or does she want me looking at something else? It seems to him that *he's* the object on display, that the dancer is free to shake or wiggle or whatever she wants, and that *he's* the one who has to figure out what he's *supposed* to want.

Which is what he's doing now, following Anna around the dressing room, watching her for some signal or piece of information that will answer the question "What does she want of me?" or more precisely, "What do I want to do so that in doing it I will have done what she wanted?" He keeps his own desires in, or down, or away from the world, preferring to want what someone else wants him to want.

And she's doing—for different reasons—the same thing, watching him for subtle clues that she can use to protect what she feels needs protecting. That's why they're both fairly quiet. It's also why they move in unison, like dancers, but haltingly, each one following the other's lead. They don't necessarily like it but there they are, going around and around in a loop, around the crowded dressing room like children in a playground.

He's saying, "What do you want to do?"

And she's saying, "What do *you* want to do?"

And he's saying, "What do *you* want to do?"

And it seems like a highly civilized etiquette, but really it's a form of resistance.

MAKING THE WORLD

As far as we know, Orson Welles lives in this particular nightclub. He eats there, and he probably sleeps there, and it's where we see him now, in a far corner of this oddly angled room, sitting at a table, making his women.

"Women" is not the right word. They're not women.

What he does is buy up boxes of plastic soldiers, gray or

silver little men in uniform, and it doesn't matter what war they were in, they're all doing basically the same thing: throwing grenades, shooting guns, slicing something with a bayonet. These are his people and what he does, he keeps a candle burning on the table and he sits at his table and takes a soldier and holds the little man over the candle flame, keeping the little arm or hand or gun close enough to the flame so that the plastic begins to thaw and melt and then drop, and he lets it drop; when it's ready, he lets a drop fall onto another soldier. He holds that other soldier under the first one and lets the drop of wet plastic fall on the breasts of the soldier below. He's making breasts.

Very carefully, dripping the arms of the plastic men, drop by drop, he creates the breast nodes, building up incrementally the rounded curve of the female breast. Each arm makes about one and a half breasts so sometimes he uses the head or the leg or a piece of artillery. Parts like the head are hard to control, and sometimes from the head a drop falls and spreads over an entire chest. That's not good. That recalcitrant soldier has to be thrown away. That soldier is a failure and he can't stand failure.

Which is fine. He has plenty of raw material. On his table he's arrayed a whole army of these little men, the finished ones. To finish them he takes them by the heel and dips the body in a mayonnaise jar filled with creamy pink enamel paint that he's devised for just this purpose, for the purpose of looking like flesh, or an approximation of flesh, the flesh of the skin of an actress or ballet dancer who resides in the back of his memory.

He spends his evenings like this, creating these figures, diminutive, naked-seeming and large-breasted, with traces of a molded soldier's uniform beneath the painted flesh. They're floating on his table, an ocean or sea of flesh-toned soldiers with protruding parts like women. But not quite women.

Which is fine with him. He's not interested in realism or gender, or even the finished product. What he enjoys is creating a world, a little society where everything is under control, his control. He doesn't play with these people, he doesn't caress them; he's not perverted like that. He just makes them, admiring what he's made, imagining them as characters in a movie, his movie. He writes the film and directs it.

LOVING THE CAMERA

Every so often someone comes along about whom people say, "The camera loves her." Or him. Usually it's a woman, often a movie star, and the reason the camera loves that person is because that person loves the camera.

Janet Leigh and Mike Vargas didn't make movies of each other, but they did take photographs. He took photographs of her, as a hobby, and they were nice photographs too, although she never quite felt the pictures captured who she really was. And the reason for this was that she fought the camera. The camera, or the entity of the camera-and-person-behind-the-camera, wanted her to *do* some thing or *be* some thing or act in a certain way, and she wanted to be herself. She thought it should be enough if she were just herself, so she struggled against the camera. And at the same time she wanted to conspire with the camera and ask it, "Where would you have me stand? How do you want me to look?" and "Which pose should I strike to make the picture perfect?"

It was a double struggle because, not only did she fight the camera, she also fought herself. She was in a gray zone where she wasn't doing what the camera wanted, and she wasn't doing what she wanted either.

She thought about the people who take good photographs, and they don't struggle. They just go about their business, doing what they happen to be doing, and if the camera wants to take them, fine. They don't care. And she remembered the time at the Grand Canyon when Mike and his Leica had her standing on the very edge of the canyon's precipice, looking out into the canyon, and he wanted her to look in a certain way. Well, she thought that was silly. She thought she should just be able to look at the canyon or whatever she was looking at—just do what she was doing—but when she tried to do what she was doing all she could think about was the camera.

And not just Vargas's camera. She was in a movie directed by Orson Welles and so *his* camera was also watching her, and although Janet Leigh was considered a movie star, and wanted to be a movie star, she didn't feel like one. She thought about Rita Hayworth. Rita Hayworth could take a good photograph. Rita Hayworth was someone about whom people said, "The camera loves her," and it did love her. Rita Hayworth would turn, face the camera, and because she was completely without fear, or perhaps because she was filled with fear, she was able to address the camera and acknowledge the camera and let the camera take her. She wanted the camera's acceptance and so she met the camera, which became no longer this invasive, exigent eye she had to be stiff in front of. Instead it became a thing she could love, and by loving it, she could also be embraced by it.

Janet Leigh couldn't be Rita Hayworth. But she couldn't be herself either. When she tried to be herself it was all a big struggle. She didn't want to love the stupid camera, but in the end she submitted. She said, "Okay. What do you want me to be? You want me to be sexy? Okay, I can do that." And in this way she invested the camera with desire, and her own desire was subsumed by the camera's desire, which was aimed at her. She waited until what the camera wanted was fairly close to what she wanted, and although this wasn't a perfect arrangement she could pretend to stand it. She created a kind of romance with the camera, and as long as the romance lasted she was able to take a good picture.

She would have preferred to have her own desires but they seemed, along with the happiness they might engender, far away. She would have liked to turn her attention out to the world, to the objects in the world, but she felt the force of desire so strongly directed at her, and on her, that when she tried to look out and see what it was she wanted, her desires collapsed back in, and she found herself again, the beautiful object, and because she knew how to function in that mode, that was what she did.

FERRIS WHEEL

Joseph Cotten, standing under the open sky, his feet settling into the wet gravel, looks down at a puddle. It usually seems to have just been raining in movies, especially movies set at night, and in this case it really had been raining, and looking down he sees, not a reflection of anything, but the puddle itself and the water of the puddle. He's standing near an open field at the edge of town preparing to play the role of Harry Lime's friend, and he *is* Harry Lime's friend, and if you would ask him he would say it's a perfectly fine role to play, but really he hates it. He hates it because he feels diminished. And he feels diminished because Harry Lime is always right. Harry Lime has a game leg—the source of his inspiration—and in the presence of that inspiration there's little room for another person. Which is why Joseph Cotten resists it.

And yet, as if he has no choice, there he is, walking with Harry, following Harry to the famous Vienna Ferris wheel, stepping into one of the enclosed compartments. And as the wheel turns, and the horizon slowly lowers below them, although there are benches on both sides of the car, the two men stand. And you can recognize Harry Lime by the confident twinkle in his eye. There's still the twinkle. But now it's a little faded, and the confidence is tinged with the fear, or the suspicion at least, that the story he's in is veering out of his control. He's not quite ready to give up that control, or pass it to someone else, which is why, uncharacteristically, he tells the truth.

He says that sure, he probably took some so-called innocent people out of their misery and grief, and as he waxes on about the wasted effort of human life, Joseph Cotten, standing under the strange moving shadows, is trying not to listen. It's impossible to close one's ears but that's what he's trying to do. It's why he keeps his eyes averted, focused not inside the cage but out, to the river and the city, and the insignificant specks moving like people in the predawn darkness. He's trying to resist Harry Lime, and yet at the same time, standing in front of Harry Lime, he couldn't not feel the centripetal pull of the man, and partly he didn't want to. Joseph Cotten *wanted* to feel what it made him feel because it was good.

And so the old habit asserts itself, of love, or affection, or remembered affection, and as he looks at Harry Lime, at the bloated version of the onetime boy wonder, he can see behind the facade of power, behind the wet cigar and the mumbling, to a man who might not actually want that power, to a man who might crave some simple affection and sympathy. He sees a man, neither repulsive nor attractive, and Cotten would like to stop resisting. He would like to reach out to the beautiful, sad, terrible man he knows is there because he knows it's not that terrible. He keeps telling himself it's not that terrible. But he doesn't reach out.

And part of the reason he doesn't reach out is his fear of Harry Lime. In the face of that fear Joseph Cotten is unable to move, not knowing what to do and afraid, if he tried to do something, if he tried to use his own volition, he'd be wrong. So he's stuck. On the one hand he would like to surrender everything, so that everything, including himself, would be under control, and on the other hand he refuses to surrender. He wants his world to change, and in fact he's waiting for that change, for some signal or sign or something to happen.

And that's when Harry Lime unbuckles his belt, pulls down his pants, and reveals the famous wound that made his game leg game. Although the sore itself is nothing more than a bad scar, by revealing it he's trying to reveal a part of himself, trying to create an intimacy, like cell mates have, or like husband and wife. If being wounded and hurt is a way to win affection, then that's what he's willing to do.

He does what he thinks is necessary, and then, as the metal cage begins its slow descent, he pulls his pants back up. And you can see Harry Lime, smiling and hopeful, his pants buckled, and you can see his big arms open, just slightly, as if he half expects or half wants, not a hug, but the outcome to change, as if he too wants to leave behind the necessity of who they are and join in some imagined embrace that would assure him the love and allegiance he craves. But Joseph Cotten doesn't step forward. They don't embrace.

BAD REVIEW

Prince Hal and a friend are drinking in the nightclub, empty now except for the hostess behind the bar, and they're having a great time, talking about Falstaff, laughing at his foolishness and his girth and his irredeemability. Hal is sitting at a table, and he begins writing on a sheet of paper, making a list of the old man's faults, and partly because they're both young and partly because the joke is between them, they feel at liberty to tell the truth. And it *is* true. Falstaff is fat. He's selfish and domineering and the truth, even a partial truth, is intoxicating, and that, along with the wine they've been drinking, causes them, in the middle of drafting this document, to pass out, the friend on the floor and Hal with his head on the paper.

That's when the scene begins, when Orson Welles walks into the room. He goes to the table, pulls the paper from under the head of his sleeping protégé, and reads the half-finished letter. And it doesn't matter what the actual words are, because what he sees is the idea, the proposal, that he, Orson Welles, is fallible. And yes, he takes it personally because he takes everything personally. He can't just walk away. He can't just leave it at that and dismiss the words or thoughts as youthful folly. Everything he fears is documented on that piece of paper, and even if the words were full of praise it wouldn't give him what he wants, the love he wants. Nothing would ever be enough.

Because he's Orson Welles he has a built-in sensitivity to betrayal, and so he sees what he thinks has happened, that his friend, his trusted companion, has turned against him, and what he does is take the whiff of betrayal and fill himself with the pain of that betrayal. He can't stand waiting for betrayal and so he betrays himself. If there's going to be pain he wants it to be *his* pain, *his* unhappiness, an unhappiness that he controls. And because he controls it, there's an air of satisfaction and optimism as he sits down at the round table.

He sits across from the prince, takes the pen from the fingers of the prince, and there's a joy almost as he finishes the letter, describing himself in ways more devastating and condemnatory than ever his friend intended. And then he stands. He clears his throat, and in the near-empty barroom he holds the note up to the light and begins. He reads aloud what they've done to him. He's in control as he orates, the cavernous room echoing with the description of his sins, the rhythm of his voice growing grander and stronger, modulating with a roar, not of pain, but denial of that pain.

FORTUNE TELLING

Although the movie Janet Leigh is acting in is not in color, it's not just black-and-white either. It's set at night so everything's a little dark, but because it was shot in the daylight it's not just darkness. There's a method of photography called day-for-night in which the film is underexposed and filtered in a way that makes the daylight seem like night, like night with a strange full moon. The sharp, distinct, moonlit shadows are really the shadows of the sun, and the artificial lights from the cars and buildings never quite penetrate the darkness. Because it isn't darkness.

And it's in this light that Janet Leigh is walking, down a wide street not far from the central plaza. This particular town has three streets called Revolución and Janet Leigh is walking down the one that's paved, trying to shake off the now-familiar feeling she calls unhappiness. Happiness itself is not her goal. What she's after instead is the absence of *un*-happiness. That's why, when she notices an old man standing on the steps of the covered sidewalk, she stops.

The man has a small wooden cage strapped around his neck and inside the cage is a bird, a fortune-telling bird. She opens her purse, and when she hands the man a few centavos he taps his clawlike hand on the side of the cage. Inside, mixing in with the birdseed, are small, translucent pieces of paper with fortunes written on them. When the bird plucks up one of these papers the old man snatches it, and with a flourish passes it to Janet Leigh.

And as she walks, slowly now, down the street, she begins reading the fortune. She doesn't wait because she hates waiting. She wants to know, now, what her destiny will be. And although the note is written in Spanish, and although she doesn't actually speak Spanish, there's one word she thinks she understands. I should say there's one word she *wants* to understand. *Felizidad.* She knows from her experience with "Merry Christmas" and "Happy Birthday" what that one word means. Happiness. She knows the word but not the context. The fortune could be saying, "You will never find happiness," or "Happiness will always elude you," or "What is happiness?"

But Janet Leigh doesn't care. She needs to believe in the promise of the fortune, that the information on the paper, whatever it is, will give her some relief from the pressure of possible unhappiness. In her refusal to acknowledge what she's feeling, she'll do almost anything. If she needs to create a fortune and have faith in that fortune then that's what she'll do, and as she walks along she keeps thinking about her future, trying to aim herself in its direction and establish a trajectory for her life, looking for some omen that will of-

fer her security, some sign that will indicate how her particular version of *felizidad* will manifest itself.

WALKING LIKE HARRY

Anybody would be stuck, and Joseph Cotten, having resisted everything, has resisted himself into a state of complete
stagnation. Which is where we find him, standing in the
sand on the edge of the bombed-out town, not knowing
what to do, but wanting to do something, and all he can
think to do is to start walking. So he does, down the middle
of a rutted asphalt road, step after step, along the white-
painted lane marker, listening to the silences between his
steps, thinking about Harry Lime and saying, in his mind,
Harry . . . Harry . . . And it starts as an incantation, like saying—if you're thirsty—"Water . . . water . . . ," and it's not
that he can't live without Harry, it's just that with Harry
around it's easier; he has something to react against. And not
just Harry Lime. He's made the whole world into Lime,
or Lime has become his world, and walking across the
bombed-out desolation he finds himself limping, slightly.
Like Harry.

When he becomes aware of what he's doing he stops; his
usual thought process kicks in and he resists what's happening, characterizing his actions as "not him" or "false" or

"imitation only." But after a while he finds himself limping again like Harry, and again he gathers his strength to fight it. And he does. And yet walking along the deserted road, looking up at the night sky and the partial moon floating in the sky, he feels himself doing it again, and by walking like Harry he actually begins to feel a little bit like Harry. And this time he doesn't fight what's happening. This time, contrary to habit and fear—or habit *of* fear—he lets it happen. He puts his effort into something other than the habitual repetition of his struggle, and he lets confusion flow out of his mind, like water flowing out of a broken cup.

Harry Lime was big and when he did something—for instance, when he slapped you on the back—you could see and feel the force that was inside of him, not because it came out in what he did, but because it came out in spite of what he did. It was constantly struggling to emerge, and in this struggle there was a kind of intensity that most people couldn't return. You tended to get out of his way. When he was hit by a bullet the doctors said he would never walk. But he wanted to walk and he needed to walk and that's what he did. What he wanted and what he needed were the same thing. And it wasn't just walking. When most people walk, they just walk, but when he walked, every fiber of his being was involved in the task of walking. His strength and his appetites and his hatred were all walking with him. And Cotten would like to emulate that. To be like that. To live, not hiding intensity, but using it. He would like to be as strong and vital and passionate as Harry Lime, and one way to *be* like Harry Lime is to *walk* like Harry Lime. So that's what he does. On the two-lane asphalt road leading to the center of town he walks like Harry. And when he does it he can feel a kind of intensity and power come into his body, or pass through his body, and although it's Lime's vitality, it's coming out of him.

So walking like Harry he feels the vitality, which is good, but he also feels the rage, which he considers less good, and so he stops walking like Harry. And of course when he does, the vitality and strength diminish. And when he walks like Harry the strength comes back. Along with the unpleasant rage. Both things exist in him, and even though the walk is an imitation, the feelings engendered are real, strange and real, and he keeps walking like Harry, down the road as far as he can, letting exist whatever wants to exist. He's feeling light, his arms and legs swinging easily in their sockets. But he doesn't feel like limping forever, so sometimes he walks like himself. And when he does, the feelings are diminished, but less than before. So he walks, first like Harry, and then himself. And then like Harry, and then himself, going back and forth like this, in succession, until after a while he creates this thing, and it's not Harry Lime, and it's not exactly Joseph Cotten either.

FIRST DRINK

$\mathbf{F}$alstaff was not always the fat old man we think of when we think of him. He was once a handsome, even dashing man facing a world of possibility. But he resisted that world and lost that world, and now he's trying to retrieve it. And the way he's decided to do that entails the forswearance of alcohol. He's stopped drinking. Although it's hard to imagine Falstaff not drinking, that's what he's doing. And looking at Orson Welles you might just think he's an ordinary, overweight man sitting alone in a nightclub. You might not see behind the false nose and the makeup to the desperation on his face. You might not see the fact that he's trying to extricate himself from his own unhappiness.

The scene begins with him at the round, wooden table, an empty shot glass in front of him, empty because he's making it empty. He's controlling its emptiness—and himself—and sitting there, he hears a fly buzzing near his ear. He brushes it away, but the fly is persistent, buzzing so close to his ear that it's practically inside his ear, and he swats it away but it keeps coming back. He snatches it up in his hand, but when he opens his fist nothing appears. When the fly lands on the table he knows what to do, and he moves in, raising his hands and holding them slightly apart. And the gesture is unique. It's the killing fly gesture, and it's also a gesture that indicates, "About this big," or "It was so long," or "Between my hands pass palpable sensations." He's hovering in for the kill when suddenly the fly darts to a new location, circling in triangular designs above the glass of whiskey. He watches the fly land on the glass and looking closely, he can see the nearly transparent wings of the fly, and the hairs of the fly, and the tongue caressing the rim of the glass.

When Orson Welles makes the gesture again it all comes back, or comes up, or comes streaming into him. The gesture is tied to the memory of the coffin in which he put his wife. Not a real coffin. She wasn't dead yet. They were performing. They were amateur performers—he was—and she was his assistant. The big finale was his sawing her in two, and when she crawled with a smile into the coffinlike box he explained in mellifluous tones to the audience that he would cut the box "this big." Meaning the woman would also be cut that big, or that small. Naturally there was a compartment she would shimmy into, double up, and only appear to be cut. It wasn't a difficult trick except one time she only got partway in, and when Welles tapped on the box—the signal that he was proceeding—she tapped back because all she had to do was slide her one leg down into the hollow pedestal. But the panel got stuck. Her other leg was still in the part of the box that was going to be cut. She was on both sides of the line, and it was the line down which Welles was sawing, back and forth, cutting first into the wood, then into her skin, and she didn't scream and spoil the trick. She kept quiet, holding herself so pure or so concentrated. And then she passed out. And even before Welles hit flesh he felt that something was wrong. He knocked. No answer. He stopped the show. He opened the coffin and saw the blood streaming out of the open gash. And the audience ran from the tent.

That was then, and now he's here, in the nightclub, massaging his leg, thinking about his past. And that's fine except he wants to be free of the past and the failure of the past. And he thought he was. He thought it was happening, that the situation had changed and was going to be different. He thought that by controlling himself he was also controlling the world, and he wanted that control and needed that control but what he needed wasn't happening. And on his face we see the realization that it never will. And when the fly lands on the rim of the whiskey glass he kills it.

Then he takes a small flask out of his coat and pours the contents into the shot glass. He doesn't drink from the glass, but he looks at it. He hasn't had a drink in—I don't know how long, but long enough to have abandoned a particular behavior, and long enough, he thinks, for a new behavior, the *not* drinking, to have merged with who he is. But still, they say that just one drink, that first drink, they always say the first drink is the crucial drink. And it must be, because when he looks down at the shot glass, and it's empty, he pours himself another. He's relieved now, having taken the drink, and although he'd forgotten the taste, it all comes back. All the effort of not drinking disappears instantaneously, and as he looks at the ring of wetness where the glass had been sitting, it's as if who he'd been when he was sober was a lie. He can now let go of that effort and pressure and striving, and be, finally, who he was afraid of being, even if it kills him.

PASSING IN THE NIGHT

Janet Leigh wasn't getting what she wanted, and the person she wasn't getting it from was her boyfriend or fiancé. At the moment she's driving her car, the two-toned convertible, trying to find him, and a donkey had been hit by a car at the corner and a crowd had gathered to watch it die. This was slowing traffic. And as she sat in her car, trapped by the car in front of her, she felt herself bumped by a car behind her. She looked in her rearview mirror and saw Mike driving a black police sedan. She turned around and waved. But he didn't see her. Or he didn't recognize her. He was honking his horn at her as if she was someone in his way.

"Mike," she said, sitting up in her seat, calling to him, and she thought he would be saying, "Hi," or "I love you," but he was signaling her to move forward, to get out of his way. He was trying to get her to speed it up, speed it up, acting as if she was responsible for slowing down the traffic. He was on his way to solve an important international crime so he was excited, and although he was looking at her he wasn't actually seeing her.

She wanted some way to get his attention, not on her car and the fact that it wasn't moving, but on her. So she honked her own horn, at him. "It's me," she was trying to say, but when she honked at him he didn't understand, he honked back at her, so she honked back at him, and he returned her honk, angry that she wasn't moving. And she didn't want to get into a honking match, but she wanted to get him to see who she was.

And it wasn't that Vargas didn't notice her. It was that to him she was merely an impediment, a thing that happened to be in his way, and so he kept trying to get around her. He had to find some thing or some one responsible for what he imagined was happening, and he didn't want to look too closely at what that thing might be. Anything that wasn't related to the top-priority crime he was solving didn't penetrate his filter of awareness, and when the lane to her left cleared up she watched him turn his wheel and pull his car up next to her.

"Mike?" she said, into his open window.

She was no longer in his way now and so he was looking, not at her anymore, but straight ahead, at something new that was in his way. There had to be something in his way. He considered that his fortune. And as she called into his open window she knew he was hearing her. And he did. He turned and faced her, and for a brief but focused moment he looked directly into her eyes. But that's all they were, a pair of eyes. There was no recognition.

And we can sympathize with Janet Leigh's frustration. She wanted to be seen as a certain type of person, a person capable of happiness, and even though she probably *was* capable of happiness, she wanted to *act* like someone who was. And that's when she made her decision.

"Susie?" Vargas said, but she wasn't listening anymore.

She was determined to jettison everything that didn't contribute to her happiness, and the person she'd always thought she loved, and did love still, was not the person she was staring at. Or if he was the same person it didn't matter because now she was different. And she turned away.

"Wait, Susie," Vargas said, but the answer he got was silence. And yes it killed her, and it might've been killing him as well, but she needed to believe that something had changed. She took a mental picture, one last snapshot of Vargas to remember him by, and then the traffic cleared. She was looking at him as he drove forward, into the city, and then she turned her car around. First she gunned the engine. She said quietly, "I love you" into the widening gap between them, and then she turned the wheel and drove away.

FOOTPRINTS

Lev Kuleshov was a Russian filmmaker who, in 1920, when he was teaching at the Moscow Film School, came up with a little experiment. He had some leftover footage of an actor's face and he showed people that face. First he showed them a shot of a bowl of soup and then he showed the face and the people thought that the man was hungry. They could see, or thought they could see, the desire that was inside of him. When the same face was shown after a shot of a woman in a coffin the people saw his sorrow. They created stories about the death of the man's mother. And when the face was juxtaposed with an image of a young girl playing with a small toy the people could see the joy that was in the man's heart because it was showing on his face.

Whether it was or wasn't.

And it works the other way too.

Looking at Joseph Cotten you don't see all the emotions boiling inside of him. You probably assume he's just a guy standing at the side of a desolate road, thinking. He's got a furrowed brow, a book in his back pocket, and the obvious destruction around him. And it's only when you take away the book and the destruction and the thoughts in his head that you see him as a man about to kill his hero.

The next scene is the scene in which he meets Harry Lime in a sewer and shoots him.

But he doesn't know that now. At the moment the future is far away, and the past is also far away. At the moment he's walking through the night, walking without direction, following the wind or the sounds of voices or the smell of something not yet burned, wandering until he finds himself standing at the edge of an open, treeless field, filled with the rubble of the city. It's flat enough and dark enough so that the stars in the sky seem to speak of possibility.

At least to him.

He's standing there, at the edge of town, looking out into the night, the dry wind blowing through his ears. The moon is in the sky and he feels its heat on his face. And he accepts that, yes, he is afraid, and when he does he feels a lightness in his body. When he looks down he sees a set of footprints in the sand, a spot where he probably stood before and he goes to that spot and puts his feet in his own footprints. The person then had been worried about what he would say or how he would act, and now he's feeling rocks through the soles of his shoes. And it's a human dilemma. Not rocks, but once we think we know who we are, to change who we are means giving up what we love, even if we hate it. Standing under the clear night sky, Cotten feels a degree, not of liberation, but of the world weaving itself around him and through him. And as he steps out of the footprints, the flat gravel isn't asking him to be any kind of person. Nor is the moon. And the question he's about to answer is, When he finds himself in a world that knows him as a certain kind of person, will he conform to the view of that world, or will he create a place for the world he's feeling now? And at this moment he doesn't know. He doesn't know if his new world will survive, or become just another auspicious beginning, fading away into the numb repetitive past.

BROKEN HEART

At the end of the movie, Prince Hal, who has now become King Henry, turns to his old companion, Jack Falstaff. I should say he turns *away* from his old companion, his mentor and guide through a life of profligacy and decadence and debauchery, and it could have gone on forever except that Hal, when the moment comes for him to assume the mantle of kingship, turns to Falstaff and says, "Presume not that I am the thing I was." He sees Falstaff, not as the benevolent rascal he always seemed to be, but as a monster, albeit a beguiling one. He says he had a dream and that the dream is over and being awake he despises his dream, meaning he despises not only who he was, but also the man still holding out that dream as a possible way of living.

And when the newly crowned king says to Falstaff, "I know thee not, old man," I think Falstaff probably saw it coming. He knew he would be forsaken. Which is not to say it doesn't hurt the old man. When his friend—his almost son—disowns him, he's devastated. He doesn't want it to happen, it's just that he knows where the story of his life is going. It's why, in one of the sources of the film, he dies of a broken heart.

But not a simple broken heart. It's both that he doesn't believe this thing is happening, and also, that with his arrogance or confidence or unwillingness to comprehend, he's made it happen. It's hard to see any regret or bewilderment on his face, but behind the showman's grin, beneath the carapace of his own importance, I believe he knows the future is lost, that Hal is gone and that he has nothing. You get a glimpse of it when, as his old friend walks away, Welles momentarily stumbles on one of the steps of the makeshift set. But just momentarily. He stands up, regains control, and smiles. And although he keeps his optimism, or mask of optimism, he knows his days are numbered. He sees the end of his life, and sees what his life has become, and he sees he has no choice. He accepts what's happening because he has to. He's the one who demanded that it happen.

NARROW ROAD

1 . BASHŌ ON THE NARROW ROAD

The morning sun rises over the still lake and Bashō, the poet, opens his eyes. He's a haiku poet from seventeenth-century Japan and he's sitting on a hard pillow in his hut near the outskirts of Edo watching a camellia bush trying to bloom. He writes a poem about the flower on a piece of paper, but it's not a very good poem so he rips it in two. Because he's leaving on a long journey his mind is distracted by thoughts of the open road. He places the poem into the fire, closes his eyes, and listening to the paper burning in the flames, he imagines the serenity of traveling. At that moment it seems to him there's nothing but peace in the world.

And then he hears the voices. In the distance his friends are preparing his farewell party, laughing and celebrating, and although a moment earlier he'd been alone and happy, now he's shivering and nervous. Unlike Li Po, the wine-drinking poet, he's sober and serious, and when he hears the hum of talking coming toward his hut his impulse is to hide. His poetry and his life are predicated on concentration, and in an effort to avoid any impediment to concentration, he

1 6 3

slips into his sandals, steps off his porch, ducks behind a juniper bush, and sneaks out along the edge of the pond. He's crawling on his hands and knees through the wet sand as quietly as possible. But not quietly enough. Some geese floating along the shore start honking at him, and when he tries to crawl away his sandal dislodges in the mud. He doesn't have many possessions and the sandal is one of his favorites so he looks around, finds a banana tree frond on the ground, and with it reaches out to pull the sandal, which is now floating on the water, back to shore. But in doing that, he splashes the water, pushing the sandal farther out toward the geese, who are still honking, and his friends, hearing the commotion, move in his direction. He abandons the sandal, squeezes through a bamboo thicket and sits in the middle of it trying to be still, trying, literally, to be one with the bamboo so that he might seem to be a bamboo reed himself and disappear. Feeling slightly ridiculous, hiding from his friends, his heart pounding in his chest, what he's done is taken the distraction he was trying to avoid and made it his whole world.

As his followers converge on him he realizes that there's nothing to do except stand up, so he does. When his friends see him they call to him, "Mr. Bashō, Mr. Bashō," and he walks to them, waving and limping, limping because of his missing sandal. They surround him and talk to him and yes, he talks to them, but his mind is on the open road. He thinks of it as a *narrow* road because on one side there's distraction and on the other side there's also distraction. He wants to find beauty and harmony, but something is always distracting him—people usually—pulling him off the road. He feels he can't really be himself around people, and it's not that he wants to be himself, he wants to lose himself, which is why he puts on his boots and starts walking. There's only one way out of the compound and so he moves through the gauntlet of his admirers as quickly as possible, bowing and saying good-bye and getting out on the road, alone, where he can finally feel free. Bashō would like to avoid the feeling of being pulled, and the force of that feeling, and to fight that feeling he begins his journey. His plan is to get first to calmness, then awareness, and then the happiness of opening himself to the world. And since he can't wait for that, he leaves before his traveling companion is ready, starting off alone, walking down the road.

"Afoot and light-hearted I take to the open road, healthy, free, the world before me, the long brown path before me leading wherever I choose." That's Walt Whitman, and although it's not a haiku, Bashō has a similar reaction, walking over the uneven earth, the chrysanthemum petals falling, and his confusion also, falling away. Not falling so much as lifting, like the mist itself evaporating, leaving him aware of his feet, one after the other, hitting the brown dirt. The road turns into a trail, the city recedes, and there he is, marginally happy, somewhat calm, his arms light, his nostrils cold, the blood flowing into his fingers. Finally on the road, the morning sun beginning to warm him, he feels a degree of peace.

2. JOHN KEATS DOESN'T KISS FANNY

John Keats was a poet who died when he was twenty-five years old. He wrote poems, and he also wrote letters, and it's from his letters that we know he wanted a girl named Fanny Brawne. He said to her, "I cannot exist without you," and "I cannot breathe without you," and I imagine his feelings were at least partly sexual. There's the admiration and friendship and respect, but there's also this other thing, the sexual thing, and that was the thing he was feeling, walking along with Fanny in the north part of London.

This would have been around 1818 or 1819, and there was probably a mist hanging in the air, probably the smell of coal fires and horse dung as they walked to Hampstead Heath, alone, in the middle of the late afternoon. I say middle because he felt that it wasn't the end, more like a prelude, that they were in transit to a place, an eventuality, her front door, where something else would happen. In his letters he never mentioned her breasts or the inside of her thighs but I think he was picturing Fanny, standing in front of him, naked and exposed. She was young and charming, and as they walked along, holding hands, he was thinking, as she was, of what was *going* to happen, later.

Another thing we know from his letters is that he wanted to be true to himself, true to his imagination and his senses, and to what was actually happening. He said that the poet has no identity, meaning that the poet becomes part of the world and sees the world through the eyes of the world. So that's on the one hand. On the other, there's desire and gratification and pleasure, and he wanted the first thing, to live the life of a poet, but he still felt the other thing. And looking down as their separate feet hit the ground, listening to the rustle of her dress, his thoughts were not the thoughts of a poet, they were the thoughts of a man in love, flying to arrive at the place where her cheeks, red from exertion, and swollen, and her lips, also red and swollen, and moist, would be waiting for a kiss. He would feel then what was beyond imagination.

Or at least beyond *his* imagination. Fanny had her own ideas and her own imagination, and because she wanted to be wanted she ran ahead along the trail hoping he would follow. She said something like "Catch me if you can, Mr. Shakespeare," and she ran over a small bridge. Keats, by that time, was already dying of tuberculosis, but still he tried to follow her. The heath was green and open and the wooden bridge she crossed was high enough so that she disappeared over its rise, and as he started to chase after her his head began to spin, the blood draining from his brain, and he stumbled into an area of grass near a tree and dropped to his hands and knees. His body was hot and shivering and he crawled to the water, to the slow-flowing stream along the edge of the grass, and with one hand he splashed water up into his face. He looked down at his distorted reflection but he didn't need the reflection. He realized he was dying, that soon he would be dead, and so he stood up. Fanny was waiting behind a bush, and he gathered his strength, crossed the bridge and found her.

The walk from there to her house was quiet. Maybe they held hands, but I don't imagine they spoke. When they stepped up to the door, they'd arrived at the place they'd been dreaming of, the moment when all the passion and desire they were feeling would express itself. The future was over because this was the future, this was the point at which fantasy met the world, and so he looked at the girl, and yes, he saw her, and he saw his desire, and he felt what he was feeling. And at that moment a kiss wasn't what he was feeling like. The thing he'd been dreaming of was one thing, and now, standing in front of his true love, what he felt was something different. And he couldn't lie. He could lie, but he didn't want to. He wanted to stay on the road of truth, even if it changed direction. When he looked at her he didn't see a beautiful girl, he saw a human being, a woman, the person he loved, and he held her hand, and felt it, in his.

Which was fine, for him. But Fanny wasn't a frozen figure in a toga running around an ancient urn. She had dreams, and now, at the moment they were about to make themselves manifest, they evaporated. Now, when he was supposed to take her and kiss her, when any ordinary man would hold her in his arms and press against her warm, soft body, he didn't. And she was disappointed. It wasn't what she was imagining, and although Keats had told her that "the poet has no identity," at that moment Fanny Brawne is wishing that the particular poet standing in front of her did.

3. BASHŌ AND THE SORA-NATURE DICHOTOMY

Bashō the poet isn't alone on his pilgrimage to the deep interior provinces. Sora, his traveling companion, the one who'd been shaving his head when Bashō started out, has now caught up and they're walking together. Part of their pilgrimage consists in visiting a number of shrines and monuments, and although Bashō prefers traveling alone, he needs someone along to help cross over streams and gather wood, and with Sora, he thinks he can be physically proximate but mentally on his own. Climbing a trail leading up through pine trees and ferns, past a blue mountain lake, Bashō is attempting to establish a solitude by ignoring the person walking next to him.

When they arrive at the stone structure marking this particular viewpoint it's already dark. They set out their bamboo mats, start a fire, and drink some broth. They don't sleep because they're waiting, looking to the eastern horizon, waiting for the sunrise and the decisive moment of the morning. Bashō is dreaming of a moment when all distractions fall away and he can experience the harmony of nature, including the nature of his own mind. That's his goal, but the only thing he's able to experience now is Sora. When he opens himself to the world, Sora is already there, supplanting that world, and there's no space for anything but Sora—Sora making tea or Sora cleaning a pot or Sora breathing through his congested nose. There's Sora on the one hand and nature on the other and Bashō would like to rid his mind of Sora. He knows the mind is a road along which a succession of objects come and go, and that he's responsible for putting Sora in the spotlight, for making Sora a gigantic distraction, and he tries to stop. He tries to change what's happening. But because Sora's been sick lately and unable to completely control what's happening in his body, at a certain point in the middle of the night his stomach begins to growl. And of course this drives Bashō crazy. Sora, who admires Bashō, is embarrassed by his outburst, but because he doesn't know what to say, he's silent. They both are. And they spend an uncomfortable night like that, sitting, listening, waiting for the next occurrence, and any thought of nature and the beauty of nature is far, far away.

In the morning, as the sky begins to lighten, there they are, boiling water, making tea, warming their hands on their cups. The actual moment when the sun rises is exactly that, a single moment, and it could well be an endless moment, certainly it's a crucial moment, and that's why Bashō is watching his breath. If his thoughts turn to Sora he tries to note them and let them go. Except for the occasional wind stirring the trees it's quiet, and Bashō is able to hear his own breathing. Except for Sora adjusting his position it's almost completely still, and although Bashō isn't looking at his friend, if he did he would see Sora's face contort in a kind of agony. Sora's ailing stomach is causing him pain, but his agony is caused by his effort to preserve the tranquillity. For

Bashō. Which he does for a while. But at some point the pressure builds up and, against his will and desire to stop it, he farts. Bashō, whose mind is already fixated on Sora, now turns to Sora, and of course the sun doesn't stop rising, so he quickly turns back to the view, to the imminent rising of the sun. He turns his body back but not his concentration. He's nervous now, feeling not quite ready. He would like the sun to stop moving, and because it doesn't stop moving, he begins to lose the stillness of the morning and the stillness of mind, and as the sun cracks the morning sky he sees it, and he tries to open his heart to what is happening. He tries to experience as completely as he can, the world. And he does. To some extent. But not to the full extent. Because he's distracted he's not actually paying attention, and because of that he's not really there.

4. PERFORMER'S DILEMMA

In the world of fashion, the photographer is king. And at the moment the king hasn't arrived. This particular photographic session is taking place in a restaurant that's been cleared of customers. The tables are bare except for one small table against the wall. Lights are shining on this table and pacing back and forth in front of this table is a model, wearing a gown, waiting for the photographer. Her name is Lisa Fonssagrives, and this would be about 1950 or a little before 1950. She was from Sweden originally, went to Paris to study dance, posed once in a hallway in a hat, and before she knew it she was a fashion model, and at the time of this particular "sitting" she's established and sought after. The reason she's sought after is her ability to be herself, to radiate what she calls energy into the lens. And not just the lens.

The whole room is giving her attention, and she's happy with that attention, and when she pushes away a loose strand of hair, everyone is watching because her every movement is effortlessness and graceful. Because she's the object, and they all believe in the philosophy of the object, she is a kind of goddess, and while they don't worship her exactly, they let her sit in the middle of the leather banquet, surrounded by men, all drinking wine or champagne. She's not drinking because first of all she doesn't drink, and also she's thinking about the photographer. Irving Penn is a famous photographer, and when he finally shows up everyone turns in his direction. As does she. That's nothing new. What's new is that she cares. Normally she's completely disinterested in who is watching her but now, when the photographer tells her to sit at the table and imagine herself in love, she tries to do what he wants, tries to do the right thing. Suddenly there's a "right" thing, and it's not her thing, certainly not a natural thing, or an effortless thing, and it's a thing she doesn't understand.

She's sitting at the table, the camera—and Irving Penn behind the camera—focused on her, and when she tries to radiate energy into the lens, or anything toward the lens and the man behind it, nothing happens. She's frozen. Her natural ability to be herself evaporates, like a mist, and although there is no mist, she feels exposed and awkward. Her hair is cut in a hairdo à la Hamlet and she tries pushing away the loose strand of hair. She tries touching her finger to her mouth. She does all the things that normally facilitate happiness but everything she does seems forced and artificial. She pretends to have a particle of dirt caught in her eye, and that's the problem right there. She's pretending. She's pretending because she's holding something back. Some part of herself is in love with the photographer and she's holding that back.

She steps away from the table. She's a dancer, and because her body is her vehicle she stands at the table and stretches her neck from side to side. She lifts her long arms out and over her head and, feeling her body and the muscles of her body, she begins to feel better. But when she sits back down, with the cup and the creamer and the white linen tablecloth, her hands, with their long, delicate fingers, are slightly damp. They've never been damp before or needed to be damp before, and why are they worried about the right thing now? She's the model. She's the one they're looking at, and she tries to believe that nothing has changed. An open bottle of dry champagne is on a nearby table and she pours herself a glass. When it's gone, she pours another glass and drinks that. She waits for the fog or shade or wall to lift, for the longed-for equanimity to return, and when it doesn't, she feels a degree of panic. Irving Penn, oddly handsome, is kneeling in front of her and she's trying to talk with him and laugh with him, and normally there wouldn't be a problem, but now, even in this casual situation, she feels herself clinging to his attention and she doesn't want that. She wants to let go of that. She's smart enough to want to be free of the influence of another person, and in an effort to find that freedom she goes, alone, to the bathroom. She says she has to "freshen up," excuses herself, and wafts like a scent, away from him and the lights and the people. The hum of talking fades away and she finds herself in the white-tiled, brightly lit chamber where there are no eyes to perform for. It's quiet here, with the door closed, and feeling alone, finally, she waits for some peace. She's waiting for a little happiness but instead of being happy, she's lost.

5. A GIRL CAN'T GO ON LAUGHING ALL THE TIME

The problem Lisa has is an old one. She's in love. It's beginning to dawn on her that she cares about Irving Penn, that she likes him, and if desire is the root of suffering then her particular suffering stems, not from wanting him, but from wanting some reciprocity. She's on a kind of road; on one side are her feelings for this man—what I'm calling love—and on the other side there's desire, the wanting to be wanted, which, like all desire, is freighted with anxiety. And

174

because she doesn't want anxiety, she pushes it away, or tries to, and in the process pushes everything away, including the love. Although she would like to have the one and not the other, the two things are joined, and so she pushes away both the anxiety and the thing she wants.

She's standing in the bathroom, looking at the tiles which are white and the floor which is tiled and white, and she's not looking at the mirror because, instead of seeing herself she wants to *feel* herself. She wants to find something true inside of herself. But she hasn't been alone in a long time and when she tries, without the attention of other people focused on her, she's not sure where to look. All she feels is dizzy, and so she walks into a stall at the end of the row of stalls and she sits on the lid of the toilet. She closes her eyes, imagines herself back in the restaurant, at the small table, and Irving Penn is standing in the dark, the camera raised to his eye. She's sitting, her legs crossed, moving her foot in circles, effortlessly radiating beauty and truth, with Irving Penn taking picture after perfect picture. They fall in love, and she imagines getting married, or being married, and living with him in a large house on an island, with several small children running along the beach.

Which is fine, for a fantasy, but when she opens her eyes the tranquillity of the distraction disappears and she's left again with the dizziness, which has now spread to her belly, which is why she stands up, turns, lifts the lid of the toilet, raises the beautiful white gown, and kneels in front of the toilet. She would like to push the dizziness away from her or out of her, but her body is not just a thing to hang clothes on. It has ideas of its own and when she places her hands on her thighs, bends forward, and stares into the clear water of the toilet bowl, her body does what it wants. Which is nothing. The relief she was expecting doesn't materialize and there she is, gazing into the reflectionless water, feeling the rebellion in her body. And I would like to say that eventually the feeling goes away, and I will, because it does. And I would like to say that everything changes. I would like to say that she sees the suffering at the root of desire and is able to transcend that desire, but the feeling, whatever it is, comes back, and although it's not what she wants, she feels it. And then it goes away. It comes and goes, and kneeling on the white tiles she watches it come and go, and then she stands up. She steps out of the stall, washes her hands in the white sink, dries them on a white towel, and then she walks out of the bathroom. First she fixes a strand of hair with her fingers, and then she walks out into the empty room.

6. FANNY EATS A BISCUIT

Fanny Brawne is not in a bathroom. She's in the kitchen, walking across the floor, carrying a tray of tea and biscuits into the wood-paneled parlor. She sets it beside a letter opener on a small table and John Keats is watching her. He's sitting on the tufted sofa, and although it's not possible to see death or the reality of death, death is pushing him on his way. He's chosen his way and his way is to look into her eyes and let whatever he is radiate into her. Whatever his feelings are, he makes no judgments about them, makes no effort to better them or redirect them. And Fanny has a problem with that. Not in theory, but in practice. Sitting there under the moose head on the high-backed sofa she's not being kissed. Again. She wants attention in the form of a kiss. That's why she's stirring the tea in her cup. There's no cream in the cup, or sugar, but she's stirring it with her spoon. Forget about reciprocity. She would like to know, not fantasy, but what is actually happening. Love means nothing unless it can be felt, and she hears his words which sound like the typical words of any lover in the world, and she sees his sickly, tender face, but she's not feeling anything. Nothing is radiating from him to her. That's why she's rearranging the biscuits on the silver tray. It's why she stands up and, using a set of tongs, tries to take hold of one of the biscuits and put it on his plate. "Another biscuit?" she says. But he doesn't want another biscuit, and that drives her crazy because they're perfectly good biscuits. He's sick, and he ought to be eating, and he's not doing what he ought to be doing. "Don't you want a biscuit?" she says to him, and when he shakes his head he seems far away. Somehow she's made him far away. And partly she wants him far away. "Fine," she thinks. He might as well be far away for all the good he's doing. And yet she also wants to be kissed. And the only way she's going to be kissed is if he moves closer or she moves closer, and she thinks about reaching out, taking hold of his shoulders, and pulling him toward her. But she doesn't. If she were on a road she would be walking between two things, between wanting him close and wanting him far away, and a person wanting disparate things doesn't see what's happening. She doesn't see that the opposition is inside of her, pushing and pulling, and so she takes a biscuit in the silver tong, and leaning into him, she holds it in front of his face, and when nothing happens she pushes it *toward* his face, aiming at his mouth. He puts up his hand, holding her wrist, and in her struggling, and her desire to stop struggling, she squeezes the tongs, thereby squeezing the biscuit which shatters, breaking into several pieces and falling onto the floor. Still holding the tongs, she kneels down—Keats is looking at her and she sees that he's looking at her as no one has ever looked at her, and she lets herself be looked at—she kneels down, picks up the pieces of biscuit, places them in her open hand, and instead of setting them back on the tray, she takes one and eats it. One bite. She swallows. And then she takes another bite. She eats the rest of the biscuit, sets the tongs on the silver tray, sits back down on the sofa, and looks at John Keats.

7. BASHŌ FEEDS HIS FRIEND

A crescent moon was hanging in the western sky as the two men stood on the narrow trail at a place where it opened up. Sora knew his birds and usually stopped to listen, but now he was stopping because he couldn't go on. His illness was serious and this was for him the end of the road. It wasn't drizzling now, and although the ground was wet, the sky was clear. The afternoon light was yellow on the hillock, passing through the yellow leaves, and Bashō was looking for the temple. They'd come to an ancient temple and Bashō was wanting, not oneness, but a little interaction with nature. He was hoping the temple would bring him some peace, but the temple was ruined, and had been for years. Instead of peace, all he found was another shrine and another failed attempt to find solace.

He wanted to start out walking again, to get on the open road again, but because of Sora's sickness he sat on an old stone of what would have been the wall of the temple and looked across the swaying trees, and between them, to the distant mountains. His plan was to empty himself, to radiate out into the world and then let the world flow into the vacuum. So he sat on a rock, and like Li Po, he sent his attention out to the world, but nothing came back except an echo, nothing but himself, no beauty, no nature, just himself as always, and his repetitious mind. Not that beauty had gone anywhere. What went somewhere was his willingness to look. The mountains were there in the distance, and the trees and the moon, but he wasn't with them. He was spinning around in his own mind, locked he felt, forever. Sora was lying by the ruined wall of the temple, covered in blankets, the satchel under his head, but Bashō didn't notice. All he could see was a leaf, one single leaf in front of his face, dangling on its branch in the wind. It wasn't dancing, or waving; the leaf was not communicating. It was just a leaf, and Bashō watched it fall to the ground.

Although it wasn't cold, Sora, lying on his mat, was shivering, and Bashō gathered some twigs and sticks and with them he built a fire. He set a kettle on the fire to warm some water, and when the water was hot he poured it into a small bowl. He added some paste, stirring it in, watching the solid dissolve into the water, turning it cloudy and dark. Sora, he thought, needed nourishment, and so he propped the young man's head in his lap, kneeled over him, and with a wooden spoon he lifted out some soup and slowly he touched the spoon to the other man's lips, opening the lips, and letting the warm broth drain down over the man's tongue. Sora was both shivering and sweating, his eyes closed, and Bashō covered him with his coat, wiping his eyes and cleaning the broth that had dribbled down his chin. The sun did what it did and then disappeared, but Bashō didn't notice. He lay down where he was, molding himself to his friend, under the blanket and coat. He was holding Sora in his arms, concentrating his energy on radiating warmth. He didn't notice when the fire died out, and by the time the crescent moon dipped below the treeline he was already sleeping.